P9-AOA-815

Handful of Stars

Other Books by Marie Pershing

MAYBE TOMORROW

FIRST A DREAM

Handful of Stars

MARIE PERSHING

DOUBLEDAY & COMPANY, INC.

GARDEN CITY, NEW YORK

1985

All of the characters in this book are fictitious,
and any resemblance to actual persons,
living or dead, is purely coincidental.

Library of Congress Cataloging in Publication Data

Schultz, Pearle Henriksen.
Handful of stars.

I. Title.
PS3569.C5532H3   1985   813'.54
ISBN 0-385-19838-8

Library of Congress Catalog Card Number 84-13790
Copyright © 1985 by PEARLE HENRIKSEN SCHULTZ
All Rights Reserved
Printed in the United States of America

First Edition

for
Stephanie, beloved first-born, and Dick Buehler

Handful of Stars

CHAPTER 1

From her desk in the deluxe office of Montval's social director, Ariana saw the two people leave the elevator and turn left in the direction of the exclusive resort's tennis courts. The man's sun-streaked, light brown head was bent attentively down toward his companion, and as they disappeared from sight the woman's throaty laughter echoed back to the French Renaissance décor of the hotel lobby.

Ariana winced. Ron was with Mrs. Fayette again. Her small head drooped as she thoughtfully twisted the diamond engagement ring on her left hand. The beauty of the August morning was suddenly blemished.

"Miss Radnor?" In the open doorway, hesitating apologetically, stood an elderly hotel guest, her lined face anxious. "Are you feeling well, dear? So pale—"

The honey-blonde head jerked up, and Ariana forced a smile which didn't quite reach her eyes. "I'm fine, Mrs. Barton. Sit down, do. Tell me how I can help you," she said with a calmness that was far from how she felt.

"Well," the older woman ventured, "I thought perhaps some riding would be nice. Does your office arrange that, my dear? Such lovely country, this part of Colorado."

Ariana's wide brown eyes mirrored her concern. "Horseback riding, Mrs. Barton?"

A frail hand reached out and patted the young assistant's smooth cheek. "Bless you, child, you needn't worry. I've handled horses since knee-high. Rain or shine, I rode my own mare six miles to school each day, up in Montana." The faded blue eyes twinkled. "That was well before I married Mr. Barton, of course." The late Mr. Barton of New York and Palm Beach, with his fleets of Cadillacs and Lincolns . . .

Ariana reached for her extension phone. "Let's see what's available. You'll need a corral boy, too, won't you?" She saw the resisting look on the mellow face. "Mrs. Barton, you simply must not ride out alone. It's not safe. They wouldn't allow it anyway, you know."

"I don't suppose you—?" There was a wistful sound in the soft voice.

Ariana stole a glance at her calendar. "My earliest free time this week is Thursday afternoon. Oh, excuse me a moment—stables? Would you please send a corral boy to the main lobby to escort Mrs. Barton to the stable master's office?"

She heard the clerk there gasp. "That old lady? She must be all of a hundred, and we're fresh out of rocking horses down here."

Ariana grinned. "You're going to be surprised," she murmured. She winked at Mrs. Barton and added, just before she replaced the receiver, "And save me a mount for Thursday, around two, will you? She's promised to ride out with me then."

She kept the smile on her pretty face until Mrs. Barton's trim figure, shoulders determinedly erect, departed for the stables on the arm of a freckle-faced corral boy.

"God love her, she's really something, isn't she?" the hotel manager's secretary, Lucy Welles, commented, coming into the office and collapsing on the davenport. "If I thought I could look that good at eighty!"

"You will," Ariana assured her. Lucy was her suitemate, and the girls were firm friends. "They say that blondes fade faster than brunettes, you know, so take heart."

Lucy was a tall, strikingly beautiful black girl from Nassau, with a matte complexion of Bahama brown, who often described herself as "brunette all over." "Not bad for ten o'clock in the morning," Lucy said now, her dark eyes thoughtfully considering her friend. "Ariana, you look absolutely wretched. Are you still fretting over that convention snafu? It's all straightened out. Forget it."

As if she could! Ariana had never made an error like that one in all the four years she had been assistant to the social director at Montval. Just thinking of her mistake made her ill.

It had happened about two weeks ago, around the middle of July. Incoming telephone calls about possible convention bookings always went to the general manager's assistant, Ron McLinn, but on that particular morning Ron wanted to play golf with a guest, newly arrived Anita Fayette, and the call had been directed instead to Ariana's desk.

"We'll need Montval Center facilities for about five hundred for the second week in December," the caller explained. "It's the annual meeting of the Western conference of medical technologists, and we will be wanting an auditorium for general meetings, five smaller rooms, a banquet, AV equipment, reservations in Montval itself—the works."

He said he was phoning in because time was rather short, and yes, he understood that his telephoned request must be followed up promptly in writing. "Mr. McLinn usually handles convention bookings of this size," Ariana had reminded him, "although I anticipate no problem. We'll be able to accommodate your people nicely."

That week in December was completely clear, as far as she could tell.

And then the confirming letter had arrived, and the request was for *September*, not December at all, and September had been booked solid at Montval for months and months. Peter Ashe, the manager, had been furious, and Ron himself had been absolutely livid.

Only Emma French, Ariana's coolly efficient boss, had remained calm. "Part of the blame for this goof is your own," she frostily reminded Ron, but Ariana's fiancé refused to accept any responsibility. How the entire affair was finally resolved, Ariana was still not sure.

"Well?" Lucy asked again. "Is that what's got you looking so peaked? You read last night until after two. I saw your light when I came in from my date." Each of the girls had her own bedroom, and they shared a sitting room in an employees' suite on the fourth floor of the hotel.

"How is Stu?" Ariana asked, trailing a red herring across the conversational path.

Lucy glowed. She was engaged to a U.S. Air Force captain, originally from Nassau, an instructor at the Colorado Springs Air Force Academy. "Stu's fine. What I came down about, sweetie, is this billing for Mrs. Barton's birthday dinner party last Friday. She's billed by catering for fifty guests, and wasn't it a much smaller affair than that? Ten or twelve, I thought."

"Fifteen, actually." Ariana's voice was muted and her face had gone quite white.

"But then why—?" Lucy glanced up from the slip in her hand and shot off the sofa. "Hey, put your head down. You look about to faint."

"Oh, Lucy, I'm so unhappy."

"Is it Ron?" Lucy swiftly closed the office door and came back to kneel beside the weeping girl, putting an arm comfortingly about her shoulder.

"Ron, yes. Other things, too. I don't know what's happening to me lately, Lucy. I set Mrs. Barton's party up for fifty guests. *Fifty!*" Her face was anguished. "Emma caught it just in time. We worked like mad to transfer everything to a smaller room and finished just before the fourteen friends arrived with the guest of honor. I *like* Mrs. Barton, Lucy, I wouldn't hurt her feelings for anything, you know that." She added tearfully, "I'm a one-man tragedy of errors. Nearly everything I've done lately goes wrong."

"Your love life, too, I take it," Lucy observed. "I've not wanted to ask, but recently your face has had that proud, hurt look. It's Mrs. Fayette, I suppose?"

"I just don't know. He's seeing so much of her. I thought he felt sorry for her, she's only forty and that's young to be widowed, and he said it was even harder for her, being left with the responsibility for all that money."

Lucy snorted. She asked, "And now what?"

Ariana twisted her engagement ring around her slender finger. "I wish I knew."

"Well, what I think won't make any difference, but I'm going to say it anyway. You're much too good for Ron. He's a selfish bloke, and he's got you so upset that you're not even sleeping nights. No wonder you make mistakes."

Ariana wiped her eyes and put away her handkerchief. "There. I'm all right again, Lucy." She looked at her friend. "They're not sending Mrs. Barton a bill for fifty people, surely?"

"No, of course they won't. That's why I was checking." Lucy looked out the window. Far above, a mist had formed at the crown of the tallest mountain. "Emma's still at the dentist, isn't she?" She suggested, "Why don't you have an early lunch—you need some food in you."

Ariana reached for her purse and found a comb. "Yes, you're right. I skipped breakfast this morning."

*

"May I join you for a minute?" Anita Fayette was wearing an elbow-sleeved tunic sweater over matching damask tailored pants. She had large green eyes, short auburn hair cut to the sleek shape of her head, and a rather square, determined chin; she was staring down at Ariana with a curious look that wasn't missing a single thing.

Ariana tensed, and the coffee cup in her right hand

trembled. "Hello, Mrs. Fayette. I have only another ten minutes, then I'm back on duty again."

"Ten minutes will suffice." Anita Fayette lifted a finger, caught a waiter's eye and ordered iced coffee, then turned back to face the girl, her shrewd gaze appraising. "So you're Ron's fiancée."

"Yes." Ariana's voice sounded calm.

Baroque gold bracelets beneath one elbow sleeve chinked softly. "You're young. Younger than I thought. And you're probably much too good for him anyway."

Rising anger flooded Ariana's cheeks with color. She sat up very straight. "I hardly think—" she began, but the words were lost when the other woman interrupted smoothly:

"Ron's a coward. He might never come right out and tell you he wants to be free, so I'm doing it for him." Her eyes studied Ariana's unhappy face with regret. "Believe me, if it wasn't I, it would be somebody else before too long. There's no faithfulness in the man."

Ariana seethed. "Yet you want him?"

"I want him. He is amusing—and attentive." Her faint smile stiffened a little. "And my money will hold him fast."

Ariana stared at her. "That doesn't matter to you? To your pride?"

Mrs. Fayette would not meet her eyes. "I am somewhat older than Ron," she stated with cool indifference. "And there is much to life that you haven't yet learned. We will do well together, he and I."

She reached for Ariana's left hand, and her eyes flickered over the modest engagement ring. "It is incredibly bad taste for me to tell you this, my dear, but it no longer really matters. Ron would never have settled for a quarter-carat existence with you. Nor with anyone. He yearns too much for the good life."

A stifled sound of hurt protest came from Ariana's lips.

"Don't say anything," Anita Fayette suggested. "Just

think about it for a little while and you'll know I'm right."
She rose to her feet, gold bracelets shimmering. "I'm
sorry to have hurt you. Will you believe me if I tell you
that someday you will look back on this as one of the
luckiest days of your life?"

She signaled the waiter and, with an afterdrift of
Jourdan's *Vôtre*, left the table.

Somehow Ariana got through the rest of the day. Working steadily, she arranged a bus charter tour for fifty
guests up Cheyenne Mountain to the Will Rogers Shrine
of the Sun, organized a trip on the Pikes Peak cog railway
for a group of visiting dentists' wives while their husbands
met in afternoon seminars at Montval Center, posted the
new film schedule for the coming week, found the shy
Colliers from South Carolina another couple to play
mixed-doubles tennis, and started off the bridge tournament in the Auraria Room.

At four o'clock the social director came back on duty.

"Toothache better?" Ariana asked, swinging around to
her typewriter to avoid Emma French's keen eyes.

"Much better. Dr. Welch's nurse slipped me in between
appointments." Her forehead furrowed with concern.
"You look dreadful—what's wrong?"

"Oh, I just have a—a headache."

"Mmm." Emma shot a worried glance at her young
assistant and sank down on the beige sofa. "Are you seeing
Ron tonight?" she asked suddenly, reaching for the events
calendar and studying it casually.

Ariana stiffened. "We have a date, but—" Her voice
trailed off in a little sigh. "I don't know, Emma."

Emma French suppressed a mild oath. "La Fayette was
in fine form for the Sandervelts' anniversary dinner dance
last night. All decked out in red chiffon and diamonds, and
making a good old-fashioned grandstand play for Ron."
She added quietly, "Peter and I wondered where *you*
were."

For a moment Ariana, her face quite pale, could not

reply. Her fingers riffled nervously through a handful of colorful brochures, and she bent her head, placing the leaflets in the appropriate file folders. "Ron thought he ought to escort Mrs. Fayette. She had no one and didn't want to go alone."

Incredulous, Emma asked, "You mean he told you he went in the line of duty? Oh, piffle—you're too bright to believe that hogwash. Anita Fayette's never lacked for escorts in her entire life. And if Ron is feeding you a line like that—" She stopped abruptly, biting back the words that burned on her tongue.

"Listen, Ariana," she said, leaning forward. "That woman's out to get your man, and I mean permanently. I don't know what to tell you to do, but it had better be something, and soon."

Ariana looked up, and the hurt was there in her eyes. "Too late."

"What do you mean, *too late?*"

"Mrs. Fayette stopped at my table in the Spruce Tree Room this noon." The words were barely audible. "She says Ron wants his freedom."

"Isn't that something for him to say? If it's true, that is."

Ariana fitted the last folder back into the file drawer. "It's true. He hasn't said a word about it to me, but I know it's true." A faint flush stained her cheeks. "I've known, somehow, for several weeks. The way he's been acting— I've just known."

Emma had risen to her feet and was pacing back and forth, rolling her pen between nervous fingers. She looked anxiously at her young assistant. "What do you plan to do?" she asked at last.

Ariana glanced at her watch. "We have a movie date for eight. If what she said is the truth, I have a feeling that he'll be calling soon—with some excuse or other." She closed her eyes a moment, drained of all energy, then added: "If he calls, I'll make it easy for him, Emma. We wouldn't even have to meet again."

The older woman shrugged her shoulders and was silent.

Ariana stared out the window at the lavender mountains, seeing the late-afternoon cloud shadows billow against the high peaks, watching the sky's first pale streaks of copper-rose that meant the sun was beginning to sink below the western slopes.

"Look at me, Ariana." Emma reached out her hand. "I must be honest. He's great in his job, none better, but I can't say that I've ever really liked Ron. At least, not for you. He's too much for the main chance, while you"—her smile was troubled—"you're the gentle sort who bruises easily, my dear. If all this turns out to be true, and not just Anita Fayette's wishful thinking, what will you do, Ariana? It would be dreadful if you let it break you."

Ariana's brown eyes met Emma's for a moment, and then she looked away, fighting sudden tears. "I've been thinking. I still have two weeks of my vacation coming. I'd go off somewhere, as soon as you could spare me, and I have a feeling they'd both be long gone by the time I returned." Her laughter was rueful. "As a matter of fact, wasn't Peter suggesting that I needed a holiday, after that convention blooper I pulled last month?"

Emma stirred uneasily.

Her voice strained, Ariana went on: "There's that small place in Florida on the St. James Court estate—the cottage Mother's aunt left me two years ago. Everything's been all tied up, what with courts in both Britain and our own country being involved, but the American lawyer tells me probate's now completed."

"But I thought you had leased it to that Florida professor and his wife?"

Ariana shook her head. "That was my original plan, as Ron and I didn't think I'd be needing it. And of course I couldn't sell it, except back to the estate. But there was something in the will against renting, too." She said sadly, "That's where I'll go, Emma."

The telephone shrilled, and the older woman reached for it. "Social Director's office, Emma French speaking. For you," she said in a low voice, passing the receiver to Ariana. "It's Ron."

*

Two hours later Ariana left the landscaped esplanade that circled the resort's small lake and struck out across a hillside meadow sloping upward toward a footpath that wound its way along the far side of the golf course. Her goal was a miniature plateau a short distance up the mountain, a resting place for hikers, with a picnic table and benches beside a small mountain stream.

Why Ron wanted to meet at their old rendezvous she could not imagine. "Look, it's over," she had told him, gripping the telephone hard. "All over. I'd rather say good-bye right now, like this."

"I want to explain, and I need privacy to do it. Please, Ariana, meet me up there. Don't let what we had end like this," he had pleaded, and she, numb with this new despair, had reluctantly agreed.

"I'll see you about seven, near the bridge," she had promised him.

She walked slowly now, moving up the spruce- and pine-studded slope with an even grace. Once she paused, just where the trail emerged from the trees, and her eyes searched the scene below. Looking far down, she glimpsed Dr. Waverley and his wife striding along the fairway of the eighteenth hole, followed by their caddies. The orthopedic surgeon was a champion golfer, a purist who scoffed at golf carts and insisted on playing all courses in the time-honored way. Ordinarily Ariana enjoyed watching him, for she admired the many facets of the man. But it was growing cooler now. A sundown breeze was stirring. She hurried on.

Ron was standing by the narrow footbridge. He saw her approaching and came to meet her. She avoided his outstretched hand. "Tell me what you have to say, Ron, and let me go."

He said sharply, "Ten minutes—that's all I'm asking of you. Come and sit down."

"I'd rather stand," she told him, her eyes anguished.

He regarded her for a moment, then shook his head in bewilderment and swept her up into his arms. "Oh God, I thought it would be easier than this to say good-bye to you —the times I've said good night, almost hating you for never letting me stay—I thought I could say good-bye tonight and walk away, but—" His fingers bit into the soft flesh of her shoulders, forcing her closer to him. He covered her mouth in a kiss of crushing intensity, then trapped her head against his chest, holding her close as he began to talk.

She was only half aware of what he was saying, feeling his words of explanation run off her mind like rain down a windowpane. It was just what Mrs. Fayette had said. And Emma, too. He couldn't bear to let an opportunity like this pass him by. "She's worth nine million bucks," he faltered, his eyes shining.

Ariana stepped back and stared at him.

"Well, say something, for God's sake!" His voice was brusque. "Listen," he said urgently, "we could work something out, not say good-bye at all, if you're willing to be sensible."

"Never." She looked up at him, searching the handsome face and finding no trace of the man she loved. "It's late," she said unhappily. "Mrs. Fayette will be wondering where you are, and I must get back, too."

"Wait." He reached out and grasped her wrist, turning her back to face him again, smoothing a shining tendril of her blonde hair with tense fingers. His voice held a touch of regret. "Aren't you forgetting something?"

She felt a stirring of the old magic. "Don't touch me," she whispered, resisting him, pulling free. "Good-bye, Ron."

Still he hesitated. The engagement ring felt suddenly heavy on her hand. She slid it from her finger and placed it carefully on the picnic table beside him. Her mouth trembled, and she bit her bottom lip, fighting for control so that he would not see her weep. But it did not matter, for Ron was already bending down to scoop up the ring and did not see her face.

She started back down the slope, slowly at first, her vision blurred with tears, then running—stumbling—slipping in the early dusk.

*

The next morning Emma French took one look at her assistant's face and closed and locked the office door. "Things are quiet so far, and that gives us half an hour's privacy. From the look of you, I think we're going to need it."

Silently, Ariana held up her ringless left hand. "Oh, I'm sorry," Emma muttered. "Damn the man—you've cried all night, haven't you?"

Ariana tried to smile. "Some. I'm getting used to the idea now."

A little bitterly, Emma said, "What I have to tell you won't help much either. The timing couldn't be worse."

She could guess. "Peter wants to fire me."

"No!" Emma French patted the sofa cushion beside her. "Sit down, dear. Have some coffee while I explain."

Ariana was determined not to be cowardly about this. "I wouldn't blame him, Emma, not with the errors I've made lately. That convention, Mrs. Barton's party, the Detroit executive who missed his plane out of Denver Sunday because I told him nine o'clock and it turned out to be five. You've been so patient, Emma—and this job is such a responsible one . . ."

"Yes, it is." The director's voice was crisp, businesslike. "I've never had a better assistant than you, Ariana. You're imaginative, warm and friendly, calm in emergencies, *very* able."

"Until recently."

"Yes, until recently." Emma put her coffee cup down. "Ariana, you recall that tumble you had late last winter on the ski slopes? Peter says you haven't been the same since then, that you seem to have lost confidence in yourself." Her brow wrinkled thoughtfully. "The house physician found nothing wrong then, but you *were* unconscious for an hour, dear. Well, at any rate, Peter's made an appointment for you to see some man in Denver, a specialist of some sort, to be absolutely certain there's been no damage done."

"What kind of specialist? A neurologist?"

Emma fussed with the coffee tray, rearranged the creamer and sugar. "Oh," Ariana said flatly. "A psychiatrist."

"I believe so, dear." Emma took both Ariana's hands in hers. She said gently, "It doesn't need an M.D. degree to know what's wrong with you. First love—such cruel pain when it goes awry. I tried to explain to Peter that all you really needed was a little time to get over Ron, but—"

"When is the appointment?" Ariana asked dully.

"Thursday morning at eleven. Would you like me to come along?"

"Heavens, no. I'm a big girl now, Emma, but thanks anyway. Who knows, the man might have a magic formula for heartaches and be well worth the trip. It can't hurt to try, can it?"

Unfortunately, it hadn't worked out that way at all. Ariana found the doctor to be hurried and opinionated. There was no rapport between them, and she felt helpless as a kitten fallen into a swimming pool. Fascinated, she listened to his terse explanation of her troubles. The unconsciousness after the ski slope fall, her recent really serious mistakes at Montval—all because she was subconsciously, even to the point of a nervous breakdown, trying to remove herself from a job she felt inwardly unable to handle?

What little Ariana knew about psychiatry made her certain there was no point in further discussion here. She departed as politely as she could, seething inside. Emma, she knew, would say "Hogwash!" when she told her. And Emma would probably also remind her, truthfully, that there were psychiatrists *and* psychiatrists, and that this one had merely been a poor choice.

Poor choice indeed! The man had stripped away all her self-confidence. After Ron's rejection, that was the last thing she needed to have happen, Ariana thought despairingly, turning south onto the interstate out of Denver.

She slowed the blue VW as she entered the Montval complex an hour later, turning down the spruce-lined avenue to the hotel itself. Someone with a huge tan Cadillac had usurped her space in the staff parking lot, squeezing the large vehicle in between Lucy's Mustang and Peter Ashe's white Firebird.

With a furious exclamation, Ariana drove on, her face flushed with annoyance. Absolutely everything was going wrong today! Now she was probably going to be late for that appointment with Mrs. Barton.

Impatiently, she cruised the parking lot, then drove down the service alley and around the circular drive by the main entrance, finding a slot in the visitors' area there. She slipped swiftly into the spot and switched off the motor, thankful to be back. With any luck at all she'd be only about ten minutes late for her riding date.

Gathering up her handbag, she left the car and dashed for the side entrance nearest her office. Tires screeched on pavement as a rapidly approaching taxicab applied brakes in an attempt to avoid her. Ariana neither heard nor saw the green car until it loomed up beside her. Frantic, she lunged to the left, felt impact and was thrown off, sprawling, on the side of the road, a rock sharp against her head.

She lay still, stunned. There was the sound of running feet. Voices. A woman screamed.

Hands were checking her arms, her legs . . . capable hands that turned her deftly over and gently supported her head. "No bones broken, it seems, although I don't like that swelling near her temple. There'll be a huge bruise on her right hip where the fender touched her, and she's scraped up rather badly from contact with the road, but otherwise I'd say she's probably all right. You should have her completely checked over, of course. A fortunate young lady—"

"Please, could you carry her in? There's a sofa in our office." That was Emma's voice. "She's opening her eyes."

In the crowd pressing close Ariana saw a stocky man who was shouting angrily: "She ran right out in front of me! All of you saw it. She could have been killed and no fault of mine."

Then she was lifted up and carried swiftly away, through the main entrance into the lobby, down the corridor, and laid gently on the office sofa.

"Thank you so much, doctor," Emma said, hurrying to the telephone to call the house physician. "We do appreciate your being there just then. You'll be all right, Ariana," she said, coming back to smooth a gleaming tendril of tousled hair away from the scraped cheek. "We just must check to be sure. And we'll need help with all these scrapes and bruises."

Ariana tried to sit up, but it was too painful. "Sorry . . . sorry, remember to call the stable master," she whispered, drifting off in a faint.

She came awake with a start, her head aching. She was lying in her own bed now, and it was evening. There was a murmur of voices near the window: Emma's hushed tones and Peter Ashe's voice. The hotel manager sounded angry.

Ariana felt a frozen numbness creep over her, a loneliness that clutched at her heart as she remembered Ron.

Why hadn't the green car just snuffed out her life? It would have been so simple. Who was there to miss her— *really* miss her—now that Ron no longer cared?

Ron, she thought. Oh, Ron . . .

Despairingly, she remembered the touch of his lips, the feel of his mouth against her skin . . . how he had reached out his hand to run it through her shining hair, gently at first, caressingly, and then grasping thick strands of it in his fist as he forced up her face to meet his hungry kisses.

A little sigh left her lips. Would things have been different if she—well, if *she* had been different?

"You're too old-fashioned," Ron had said. More than once he had said it, his voice scornful. "You have old-fashioned morals that don't match your beautiful body. Why won't you let me stay tonight? It's only two months to our wedding, and I go nearly crazy with wanting you."

She had tried to pull away, her breasts agitated and her brown eyes enormous. "No, Ron—we can wait. We have the rest of our lives ahead of us."

How had he answered her? "So it's 'no' again, is it?" Something like that—and now she was alone. All alone, and her body ached with the aloneness. The grief and pain flooded back, pounding at her eyes, drowning her in waves of unhappiness until she slipped again into restless slumber.

*

"Hi, welcome back." Lucy smiled at her from an armchair near the side of her bed. "You've had a long sleep, friend. Feel like a little supper?"

"No, thanks, Lucy. Well, maybe a cup of tea." Her body ached, her head was pounding, and her scalp felt dreadfully sore.

Lucy went to the telephone and made two quick calls. "A supper tray will be here soon," she said, coming back to sit on the bed. "I promised Emma I'd phone as soon as you awakened. She had to be with the bridge tournament, but it's over now and she's on the way up."

"What time is it?"

"Oh, about ten." Lucy checked her watch. "Ten fifteen."

"Didn't you have a date tonight? You're not breaking one just to sit with me, are you?"

Lucy shook her head. "Rest your fears. Stu called; he's got an officers' meeting of some kind. Mrs. Barton offered to sit with you, but I was free so we just let her in to see that you were really all right and then sent her on her way." Lucy grinned at her. "That's some woman! I do admire her. What is she, do you think, eighty?"

"Going on, I imagine." Ariana moved her body gingerly into another position. "I feel about ninety myself."

Emma arrived at the same time as the waiter with the food. Ariana saw her and began to cry. "I didn't see the car—I never even heard a car. It was suddenly just there, almost on top of me."

"Hush," Emma said. "Forget about it, dear. We all make silly mistakes. Drink your tea and then rest again, honey. You're all right. No great harm's done."

Only, harm had been done, of course. Or had she dreamed it?—Peter Ashe's low voice, harsh with irritation: "Damn it all, Emma, this is the last straw . . . walked right into that car, witnesses say so . . . just one more incident like the others she's bungled lately . . . lost her touch . . . finished the first of the month . . ."

And Emma's quiet "Do hush, Peter. She might hear. We can discuss this later."

CHAPTER 2

The flight attendants of Continental's nonstop Miami-bound flight moved up and down the aisle distributing magazines, taking drink orders, graciously answering a dozen questions as they brought pillows or located a deck of cards. One of them appeared suddenly at Ariana's side.

"Is there anything you'd like, Miss Radnor?" She dropped down into the empty aisle seat. "We'll be starting to serve lunch soon. Would you care for a glass of wine before your meal?"

Ariana smiled back at the friendly girl. "Not now, thank you. Perhaps later. You're the one Lucy Welles knows, aren't you?"

The stewardess got lightly to her feet. "Right. She asked us when you boarded to keep our eye on you . . . pamper you a little bit. I've known Lucy since the days when she was a stew for Bahamasaire. We would have bet money that nothing would ever get Lucy off flight duty, she loved flying so, but that was before she met Stuart Rolle." The pretty stewardess made a wry face. "Love. What it doesn't do to us gals."

Silently Ariana agreed.

After a pleasant lunch and two cups of rich, dark coffee, she pushed back her seat, resting her head so that she could look drowsily out at layer upon layer of billowing cloud formations. She thought that Lucy would be back at her desk by now, her dark head with its cap of close curls bent over the morning's correspondence. Emma would probably come up on her coffee break to hear firsthand how everything had gone, and Lucy would be able to tell her how composedly Ariana had boarded the plane.

"No tears," Lucy would say, proudly, and Emma would be so pleased. Perhaps Mrs. Barton would come to inquire, too.

Ariana sighed. Emma had done so much for her these last weeks. "You're *not* fired," she had said succinctly. "You're going on a three-month leave, and with six weeks' sick pay, too. Twenty-four is too young to feel as broken up as you do now. There's too much tension and heartbreak in you, dear, and you need to get away to heal and grow well. Florida's a beautiful state, and you're fortunate to own a place there to go to. You may never want to come back here, Ariana, but let's cross that bridge when you come to it in three months' time."

Determinedly, Ariana closed her eyes. If things went well in Florida, chances were that she would not return. She was going to miss Lucy, though. Lucy and Emma and guests like Dr. Waverley and Mrs. Barton. And Ron . . . But ahead was a new life—her own small cottage on the ocean, new friends, probably a new job. And someday, some far distant someday, perhaps she'd fall in love again.

Two hours later she came awake when a hand lightly touched her shoulder. "We'll be landing soon, Miss Radnor." The same stewardess was leaning over, pushing the recline button to bring her seat into the upright position. "Will you fasten your seat belt, please?" She reached up and brought down Ariana's lightweight camel-hair coat. "Do you have anything else?"

Ariana indicated her carry-on flight bag stowed under the seat in front. "Only that. You've been so kind. Thank you very, very much. When I write Lucy, I'll tell her so."

"I hear they're getting married soon. Say best wishes to her from Maggie." The girl moved on up the aisle checking seat belts.

Ariana felt the jet begin to let down to a lower altitude.

She gazed out the little window. Their plane was still over the Everglades, the great "river of grass" . . . five thousand square miles of gray-green lowlands covered with vast marshy pools, immense lagoons and bayous, oak hammocks and small, sparkling lakes with tropical sunshine glinting on the water. This was the home of egrets, eagles, all manner of waterfowl, wild orchids, countless varieties of fish, the black bear—yes, and tribes of Miccosukee and Seminole Indians, too, Ariana remembered.

As it neared the coast, the great jet banked . . . sank toward the earth . . . roared over expressways and traffic cloverleaves, over miles of concrete aprons . . . touched down on the runway with a slight jar and rolled on to a near stop, then taxied slowly to its appointed hookup position at the huge passenger terminal.

Ariana was checking her makeup as the intercom switched on and a stewardess's voice began: "Welcome to Miami, ladies and gentlemen—"

Carrying her hand luggage, her coat and her purse, Ariana left the plane through the accordian-like jetway, following the stream of passengers down the long concourse to the main lobby. At the Continental Airways' ticket counter she said: "I believe you're holding a letter for me from a Mr. Cornwell."

The airline agent checked her driver's license for identification and passed her a white business envelope from her attorney, two keys clearly outlined within its folds. Ariana signed for the hand delivery, thanked the man, and headed for a down escalator and the carousels of incoming luggage. By four o'clock she had left behind the resort city of Miami with its tall condominiums and thriving new industries and was driving north on the Florida Turnpike in a small rental car, her suitcases neatly stowed in the seat behind her.

The world seemed bathed in brilliant tropical sunshine and for the first time in weeks she felt a surge of happy anticipation.

There were two ways from the airport to the little village of Hibiscus near Delray Beach, about fifty miles north of Miami. Ariana would have preferred the coastal road, edged with sandy beaches and small resort communities, almost always within sight of the beautiful summer sea. Raymond Cornwell's precise directions to reach her cottage, however, were by way of this more inland turnpike.

To the right and left of the great highway stretched flatlands of palmetto scrub and forests of slash pine. Mile after mile. Except for the fast-moving automobiles and transport trucks, there seemed to be a world of silence around her. Ariana felt her earlier high spirits begin to droop.

At the Pompano Plaza rest area she stopped to buy a map of Florida and a tall glass of delicious orange juice. She sat on a concrete bench in a quiet spot that was shaded by oaks and palm trees and studied the map. The Delray exit was still some twenty miles ahead, and there was no sign at all on the map of a little place named Hibiscus.

The sky was overcast now, and the humid atmosphere uncomfortably muggy. Ariana slipped her hand up to lift her hair off her neck, letting the air touch the nape. Tired, hot, and perspiring heavily, she felt discouragement sweep over her. Was this what August was going to be like in the tropics?

Sipping the last of the cool juice, she reached in her handbag for Mr. Cornwell's brief note and clipped his instructions and small directional sketch to the larger map. The first raindrops were falling as she ran to her car, started the motor, and took the access road that led back onto the turnpike.

The highway loomed ahead, wet and glistening. With her hands glued to the steering wheel and her eyes straining to see through the streaming windshield, Ariana drove doggedly on. The gray sky grew darker with each mile.

Signs warned of an approaching exit. Lighthouse Point —Deerfield Beach—Boca Raton. The last name had a familiar ring. She stole a quick glance at Mr. Cornwell's instructions. Yes, she was to leave the turnpike at the exit after Boca Raton. "It will be marked Delray," the note said. "After exiting, turn left—that's east, toward the ocean—and follow my directions to reach the cottage."

Forty minutes later she drove onto the grass verge of a rather narrow boulevard and parked. According to the attorney's map, she was nearly at her destination.

Tears of exasperation mingled with the raindrops sliding down her cheeks as she left the car and splashed up to the street sign, peering at it through the deluge. Rain poured down the back of her dress and into her soaked shoes.

St. James Lane. At last!

Wind tangled her hair as she fled back to the car. Her dress clung to her, sodden against her legs. She wondered helplessly if it wouldn't have been wiser to stay overnight in a Delray motel, proceeding to the cottage in morning light. But second thoughts were too late now. She was almost home, and besides, she needed to conserve every possible dollar.

Home? She groaned aloud as she started the car, driving slowly down a narrow road overhung with rain-drenched oaks and banyan trees. The lane ended abruptly in front of a great wrought-iron gate set in a stone wall.

The barrier's closed bars offered no welcome, but in the gleam of her headlights Ariana read its painted signboard: *St. James Court.* None of the estate buildings, of course, were visible from the street.

She stopped the car, got out, and matched the heavier of her two keys to the lock. The gate swung back on oiled hinges. She looked beyond it, up the neatly graveled drive that wound gracefully out of sight around a complete wilderness of dripping bushes. In the dashboard light she checked her watch. Not yet seven. It was the overcast sky and the rain, then, that accounted for this early darkness. For the second time that day, Ariana wished that she had remembered to buy a flashlight.

She drove through, got out again to relock the gate, and fumbled in her purse for the estate map. According to Mr. Cornwell's pencil sketch, the gatehouse cottage was located by the ocean on its own half acre, and was reached by a small road on the left side of the graveled drive about two hundred feet in from the main entrance to St. James Court. She could have wept with relief when she found the place on the first try.

As she got out of the car in a tiny clearing, the rain ceased, the setting sun broke through the clouds, and there it was, waiting for her up a curving pathway—a small, low-roofed cottage built of the native cream-colored coral rock. She saw yellow shutters at the windows and a yellow dutch door, above which hung a sign that read *La Casita . . .* the little house.

For so long now she had been trying to imagine what the cottage would look like, but never had she ever dreamed it would be something as dear as this. Eagerly, she groped in her damp handbag for the keys and inserted the smaller one in the lock. The dutch door swung open, and she reached hopefully for an electric light switch.

Light glowed around her from several table lamps and from a lovely Waterford chandelier suspended from the ceiling. She was standing in a large living room with paneled pine walls and tall windows on three sides. At one end was a fireplace, its stone construction reaching all the way to the dark-beamed ceiling, and its wide hearth bright with a cluster of clay flowerpots holding exotic pink and gold and lemon-colored daisies. On the mantel rested an impressive collection of shells. French doors across the room were curtained in thick ivory silk, pulled back now so that Ariana could see a terrace deck, and beyond the deck the dark blue of the Atlantic.

There was green carpeting underfoot, a bright, cheerful green; and comfortable chairs facing the fireplace, and an L-shaped sofa, all upholstered in a textured cream brocade. Her attention was caught by a delicate satinwood writing desk and chair near the french doors. Their mellow honey-colored finish blended like grace notes with the beautiful room.

She found the bedroom next. Small, homelike, with an old-fashioned double bed and crocheted white spread, a white-painted dresser and an oval mirror framed in seashells. There was a plain pine rocker placed so that one might look straight out to sea through the window, closed and shuttered now. Here and there on the varnished hardwood floor were soft green shag rugs.

The tiny alcove of a kitchen was to the right of the entrance, and a compact, white-tiled bathroom with thick yellow towels was just beyond.

Ariana explored the kitchen cupboards and the refrigerator hopefully. Mr. Cornwell had promised basic supplies, enough to get her started, and she discovered that a cupboard shelf held tea bags, a jar of instant coffee, and a loaf of white bread. In the refrigerator she found a generous cut of Cheshire cheese, a bottle of white wine, a container of dark red cherries, and some milk.

She was suddenly aware of being hungry. Terribly hungry. She breathed a silent thank you to Mr. Cornwell or his efficient secretary. First, she would get her luggage in and unpack some fresh clothes; next, a welcome cup of tea, some cheese, and some cherries. And then—oh bliss—a shower and bed.

It had grown quite dark, and the sky was overcast again. Ariana slipped out the dutch door and down the flagstone path to the car, leaving the headlights on while she made return trips to the cottage with her suitcases.

Weariness was overtaking her rapidly now. She showered in the small bathroom, dried herself with a fluffy yellow towel, and hastily pulled clothing from a suitcase until she uncovered a white plissé housecoat. She brushed her hair, located scuffs, and somewhat refreshed made her way to the kitchen.

On the shelves of the cupboard above the small sink Ariana found glassware and china—Edinburgh Crystal in the Thistle pattern, she noted with pleasure, and a dinner service for eight in Coalport's lovely old Ming Rose china. Washing the cherries, brewing the tea, she thought of her great-aunt who had placed these things here for her.

She took the cup and a small plate of food with her out to the deck, opening the french doors and stepping out into the night. All trace of rain was gone. The tropical air was rich with the scent of flowers. Above, the moon was silver in a star-decked sky. A light breeze ruffled her hair, cooling her body in the short cotton robe.

She walked to the edge of the deck, leaning against the wood railing and looking out to sea. Her great-aunt once had written that the Gulf Stream ran close to these shores. In the starry darkness she could see the lights of a passing ship, moving north with the Stream.

She drank the last of the tea, spat the stone from the final cherry, and, exhausted to her bones, walked to the bedroom. Stripping off the housecoat, she flung the shutters wide. She had unpacked no nightdress, but what did it matter . . . the night was warm. The last thing she saw, slipping naked under the sheet, was the crescent moon.

*

Her dark dream ended in a terrifying crash and a sudden flash of light. She came confusedly awake, not knowing for a disoriented moment where she was. She sat up in the strange bed, clutching the sheet protectively across her breasts. A narrow beam of light traced its way across the living room wall. She felt her body quiver. Then the light came again, and a man's low curse.

"Who's there?" she called out, her heart beating fast.

Beyond the deck she could hear the sea. Or was it the

sound of rain? In the shadowy opening to her room she saw a dark figure.

"Please—who's there? I know it's someone."

There was the click of an electric switch, and the lamp on the white dresser came aglow. A tall, broad-shouldered man stood in the doorway, leaning against the doorframe, watching her. His eyes were shadowed in a lean, bronzed face. Dark hair curved down across his forehead. He held a bottle of white wine in one hand.

The man took a step toward her. "Join me?" he asked politely, putting his flashlight down on the dresser and pulling a corkscrew from a pocket. There was a little swishing sound and the cork was free.

"Get out!" Her voice quavered. "Take the wine and get out!"

"Back in a minute. Glasses—" he explained apologetically and vanished. She leaped from the bed, fumbled for her housecoat, and looked frantically for a weapon—the hand mirror, his flashlight, anything.

He had her camel-hair coat on one arm when he returned. "Don't be stupid," he warned, tossing the coat to her. "Put that on." His eyes swept over her tousled hair and slender young body. "Do you always sleep nude?"

There was a faint smile on his lips, and that infuriated her. She shrugged into the coat and slipped her feet into the scuffs. "Who are you? What do you want?"

He saw her tentative movement toward the living room and stepped in front of her, blocking the way. "There's no telephone," he said. "Not yet. Not since your aunt's death. Better order one in tomorrow."

She stared at him, astonished. With a slow, rather cynical smile he offered her some wine. The glass gleamed in the lamplight. "Would you like a bit of cheese with the Chablis?"

Weakly, she accepted the wine. He took her arm and steered her firmly to a chair near the fireplace. "You—you knew my great-aunt?" she asked him.

He rested his wine glass on the hearth, pulled a car key from his pocket, and handed it to her. His dark hair gleamed with raindrops. "You left your headlights burning, and the key was in the ignition," he said soberly. "That was very foolish of you."

He turned away and reached for his glass. She had relaxed a little now and was able to see him, really see him. Tall and dark, his face deeply tanned, he was clad in scuffed mocs, drenched blue jeans, and a white shirt unbuttoned almost to his waist. A man in his middle thirties, she thought . . . a man who held within himself a powerful anger that showed in his bitter smile.

Eyes of the darkest blue demanded her attention, and black brows drew together in a frown. "I came in to check if everything was all right with you. Those french doors to the sea were wide open, the curtains blowing in—everything wet. The windows in your bedroom were open too, letting in the storm. And your front door was not locked."

Her eyes were still dazed with sleep. She stammered, "I was so tired. I've been traveling for hours, all the way from Denver today. It wasn't raining when I went to bed." Her voice sounded apologetic in her ears, and suddenly she was furious, at him and at herself. "Well, it *is* my house," she snapped at him. "And you still haven't told me who you are."

Incredibly, he just looked at her, then walked to the kitchen sink, found a floor cloth and a pail, and began to soak up the damp spots on the green carpeting by the windows to the ocean. "You know your way around rather well," she said angrily, huddled down in the cushions of the armchair.

Without looking up he said, "You're Ariana Radnor, of course."

"Yes. Yes, I am." He had pronounced her first name correctly, she realized with surprise, slurring the vowels together in the soft Welsh way.

He wrung out the cloth and took the pail back to the

kitchen. She heard him washing his hands. When he came back, completely at ease, he said, "Yes, I knew your aunt."

"My great-aunt, Margaret?"

"Yes." He indicated the wine bottle. "We've been expecting you. I'm your neighbor—for the time you're here." Those deep blue eyes met hers for a moment. "Look," he said sternly, "lock up at night. It's safer. And that's an order."

She was aware of a nervous tingling down her back. This might be the caretaker cousin that the lawyer had mentioned. "Oh, you're the one who brought over the wine in my refrigerator. That's it, isn't it? I didn't think, somehow, that Mr. Cornwell ran to Chablis as basic supplies. And what do you mean—safer?"

He gave her a cool smile. It did not reach the dark blue eyes. "Just that. Safer." His hand touched her arm. "Go back to sleep. I'll let myself out. Goodnight."

She was right at his heels. "You still haven't told me your name. You're living at St. James Court? Are you related to the new owner, the Farleigh nephew?"

"You might say so," he replied, looking at her in a rather speculative way. "Do you know Sebastian Farleigh?"

"I met him once. When I was eight or so. We came to visit my great-aunt that summer."

He stated flatly, "Things change a lot in sixteen years." The door closed firmly. She heard the lock click into place.

CHAPTER 3

After the night's heavy rain, the morning was all sunshine. Ariana lay watching the gleaming dazzle of sunlit water reflected from the ocean as it shimmered back and forth across the ceiling. She slipped out of bed and ran to the french doors, pulled them ajar and stepped out onto the driftwood-gray deck. Cypress floorboards felt deliciously cool to her bare feet. A warm breeze riffled the fronds of the coconut palms that fringed the dunes. All around her was the fresh smell of earth and grass and ocean.

She watched gulls circle in the quiet morning sky, heard the calls of seabirds. On impulse she left the deck and ran barefooted, with her hair streaming out bright and free, over the pathless sand dunes starred with little yellow beach flowers whose brief lives would end by dusk. She stood on the golden edge of the sea, and lazy breakers foamed up about her bare toes. When she touched her tongue to her lips, she tasted salt.

There was a newness to this day, a sort of rain-washed, beginning-again sensation. A welcome feeling of newborn peace to her.

Picking her way carefully to avoid the dune burrs half hidden in the coarse beach grass, Ariana went back to the cottage. After she had breakfasted—coffee and plain toast at the cherry-wood table in the living room—she sat a moment, debating what to do next. She yearned to explore her domain, every inch of the cottage and then the grounds, but first she knew she ought to unpack, hang her dresses and slacks in the bedroom closet, and place clothing neatly in the trim white chest.

And, clearly, she was going to have to make a list of groceries and supplies, shopping for enough to last her at least three weeks, for she couldn't afford to keep the rental car much longer. When Lucy sent the money from the sale of her blue VW, perhaps she would buy an inexpensive good used car. If there was such a thing anymore.

She thought about that for a little while, absentmindedly noticing a water stain on the bottom of one of the long ivory draperies. That had probably happened last night when the rain blew in the open windows. And she still didn't know the man's name . . .

Ariana poured herself another cup of coffee. She drew squiggly designs on the back of her grocery list and wondered about him. Something about his dark blue eyes and black brows reminded her of Cecil Farleigh's nephew, Sebastian. Seb, they had called him—a tall, brown-haired boy of perhaps seventeen or eighteen then. He'd finished school in England that year, she remembered, and was going on to college in New Hampshire in the fall. He had seemed a man already in her eight-year-old eyes.

How long had she and her mother visited Great-aunt Margaret that long-ago summer? Perhaps a month? She was not sure. They had come down from Connecticut as soon as school was out, staying in Margaret's suite in St. James Court, and waiting for Ariana's father to find a house for them in Fort Collins, Colorado, where he had been sent by his firm.

Margaret hadn't been married to Mr. Farleigh then. She'd been his private secretary for years, though. Ariana remembered her as a slender, white-haired woman with pretty pink cheeks and a merry laugh. She remembered, too, the day her mother had opened a letter—oh, at least six years later—and said delightedly, "What do you know, Aunt Margaret's married Cecil Farleigh!"

"That old Englishman?" her father had commented. "He must be all of seventy-five."

"Well, Margaret's over sixty. And she's always been devoted to him."

"She's done well for herself," her father had answered. "The man's worth a mint. Property all over Britain, plus that large estate of his own on the ocean in Florida."

"Margaret wouldn't care two cents about any of that." And then her mother had said, thoughtfully, "Oh, his family isn't going to like this at all, are they?"

Neither of them had paid any attention to Ariana, fourteen and all ears. Her father said, "But he had no children by his first wife, did he?"

"No," her mother had answered slowly. "She was ill so long. But there were several younger brothers in England, and a heap of nieces, and that one nephew who was always Cecil's favorite of the lot."

Her parents had remembered Ariana then, and the conversation closed with her mother's worried "What on earth shall we send them for a wedding gift?"

Ariana got up from the table and carried her few breakfast dishes to the little kitchen. How long ago all that seemed now. Her parents had been dead four years already, killed in a three-car interstate pileup on their way to Ariana's college graduation. The pain of remembrance dimmed her eyes, and she walked quickly into the bedroom and touched the seashell-framed mirror with a loving hand.

"A Victorian antique," the clerk had assured them that long-ago day in the small antiques shop in Denver. "The base of the frame is sterling, and the mirror itself is in perfect condition." Her mother had hesitated, but Ariana had cried out that it was exactly right for Aunt Margaret's present.

People she loved were gone, while material things remained, Ariana thought sadly. The antique mirror, reflecting the green-blue of the sea from its shining surface, was as lovely as ever.

She moved across the room to make the bed and finish unpacking her cases. Her cheeks burned when she slid nightdresses into a lingerie drawer of the dresser, and she saw again the brief flare of interest in dark eyes before a cynical voice asked if she always slept nude.

The sun was climbing higher in a bright blue sky when she completed the lengthy grocery list and finished checking cleaning supplies. The heat of August lay heavy upon her as a thick blanket, and a film of perspiration covered her body. She thought longingly of a swim in the blue water just beyond the deck.

The pale sand at the top of the dunes scorched her bare feet as she slithered down the sloping incline to the deserted beach. Sunshine blazed down on her in her brief black bikini. She paused a moment at the water's edge, then dropped her towel to the sand and ran into the breaking surf, disappearing smoothly under a creaming wave.

The sudden coolness of the water was a delight. Ariana turned over on her back and floated, her hair streaming loose behind her in the gentle lift and fall of the waves. She saw seagulls, and watched a wisp of a cloud trail its gauze across the blue sky.

On a rock jetty by the curve of the inlet off to her left, the figure of a man stood, staring in her direction. He seemed to be waving, and with both hands now. Eyes narrowed against the brilliance of the sun, Ariana watched him for a moment and then lifted one arm in a casually returned greeting. It was too far to be certain, but it appeared to be the aggressive dark man of last night's rain storm . . . the man with the cynical look in deep blue eyes.

Quickly, Ariana turned on her side and swam in the opposite direction. She thought she heard him call, but when she looked back the jetty was deserted. She was startled, though, to see how far out she had come and turned at once to return to shore.

It was when she was still a good distance from the beach that her right leg began to ache. She turned on her back, floating for a short while, and then pulled her right leg up to massage the cramping muscles. She was determined not to panic, and when the pain eased a bit she set out toward shore with a strong crawl stroke.

Within minutes the throbbing sound of a motor startled her, and she lifted her head to see a boat with wide open throttle cutting powerfully through the water straight toward her. Frantic now, she treaded water and waved an arm to warn of her presence.

The sports boat surged closer and then swerved to one side. The motors throttled down and the fountain of crystal wake sank back into the sea. Ariana thrust her dripping hair from her face and recognized the figure in the boat. Something struck the water beside her. "Hang on! I'll pull you to the boat."

"No, I'm all right, I'm swimming in," Ariana told him. Their glances locked.

"You could have fooled me," the dark man retorted. He fastened a boarding ladder in place. "Don't be an idiot. You caught a cramp back there. Get in before you're in real trouble."

Her body stiffened in protest at his curt order, but common sense warned her to accept the offered help. She ignored the rope and swam directly to the boat, clambered up the ladder, and slumped down on the padded cushions of the upholstered rear deck.

For a moment she huddled there, more exhausted than she had realized. She was aware that he pulled in the rope, coiling it over a teak-brown arm and tossing it to one side. He said, "That was a damn fool thing to do!" His eyes glinted with contempt and the harsh lines in his face were far more pronounced.

She flushed. "I didn't ask you to come out for me. I'd have made it in okay."

He stared at her grimly. "You were in trouble and you know it. We've had shark sightings near that small reef recently. Didn't you hear me yelling my head off to warn you away?"

Her brown eyes went wide and she sat up abruptly, her lovely face quite white. With shaking fingers she shook back her dripping hair. "I heard nothing. I was so warm, and the water looked—I didn't know."

"Well, you know now. My God, girl, is life so unimportant to you that you swim alone in strange waters? You can thank your guardian angel that I went down to the jetty and happened to see you out there."

He went back to the wheel. The motors surged into life, and the 23-foot Seacraft turned to shore.

Ariana closed her eyes and crouched on the cushions, shivering with the chill that shook her body. She heard the motors die, felt the gentle nudge of the boat against the bumpers of its mooring, and opened her eyes. The man looked down at her in silence. Then he was lifting her up in his arms and carrying her down the jetty, striding across a broad expanse of lawn.

"I can walk," she protested, her eyes shut against the sun.

His voice held a gentle irony. "Oblige me, Miss Radnor, by just saying nothing at all for a few minutes."

Numbly, she stared up at him.

His long strides took them swiftly up shallow stone steps and along a wide balustraded terrace. She had a confused impression of a carved entrance, a flagstone-paved reception hall, and of being carried into a spacious drawing room. He lowered her onto a sheet-shrouded sofa, said "Back in a minute," and vanished.

He moved quietly for so tall a man, she thought wearily, shifting uneasily on the sofa and hoping the dampness of her bikini would not stain the upholstery under the protective sheeting. He was back with a startling abruptness. "Drink this."

Hesitating, she took the glass. "My suit's damp—"

"No matter. Drink the brandy. You're still chilled." He draped a woolen shirt over her shoulders, helping her arms into the sleeves. "Warmer now?"

"Yes, thank you. I'm sorry to be such a bother."

He said tautly, "Some women are born to be."

At that, she swung her feet to the floor. "You seem to go out of your way to be rude. I can't think what you've got against me," she protested. Her eyes moved around the room, observing the ornate mantel of the fireplace, the decorated ceiling and priceless rugs, the shrouded furniture. She heard herself ask him: "You're living here?"

His eyes raked over her from the top of her gleaming head to her small bare toes. "Yes, if it's any business of yours."

She felt dazed. "I don't understand—this *is* St. James Court, isn't it? It looks so—so lifeless like this. Neglected, even. I remember flowers on every table, and paintings on the walls. Music and people. Happy people—"

He said slowly, "You're remembering the Court the way it used to be." He stared out the bank of tall windows that faced the sea. "That was a long time ago."

Ariana stood up. "Well, thank you again, Mr.—? Please, may I know your name? It's awkward for me to keep saying Mr.—er."

"Farleigh."

She said gently, "You are Sebastian, aren't you? I thought so, for a minute last night, but then I wasn't certain. Sebastian would have remembered me, wouldn't he? Don't you?—remember me, I mean?"

He interrupted, "You're barefoot, and it's quite a walk back to the cottage. If you'll wait a minute, I'll get the golf cart out and run you back, Miss Radnor."

So that's how he wanted it to be. "Thank you, no. I'll not trouble you further, Mr. Farleigh."

She shrugged off the shirt, and her bare foot struck a cardboard box shoved partly under the sofa and sent its contents spilling out across the muted hues of a beautiful Bokhara carpet. Colorless plastic envelopes . . . dozens of small, empty plastic bags sliding out of a plain tan box. "I'm sorry, so clumsy of me." She bent at once to scoop the little envelopes back into their container.

"Leave it!" he snapped. "It doesn't matter." He seized her arm and steered her toward the doorway. "Things are at sixes and sevens here," he explained more smoothly, "but my housekeeper's due back next week. I'm just camping out until then, and there's stuff all over the place. She'll put things right fast enough, Meg will. Meg and Luke—do you remember them?"

"I think so, but there've been so many years between visits. May I use your telephone while I'm here? I'd like to call service and order a phone installed at the cottage."

"I phoned them yesterday. They'll be out tomorrow. Or the day after."

"Oh, good. I'm hoping to get all my errands and things done this week because I'll need to start looking for a job soon, next week perhaps."

The golf cart pulled up by the yellow dutch door and Ariana hopped out. "Thank you again, for everything." She thrust open the door. "May I offer you a cup of coffee, Mr. Farleigh?"

He said seriously, "What kind of job will you be looking for? I had thought this was to be a vacation for you, two weeks or so and then back to—Colorado, wasn't it? If it's a secretarial job you're after, I might be able to help you. I have a number of friends in the Miami area."

"Miami? But isn't that too far to drive each day?"

His glance was sharp. "You surely didn't intend to stay on here?"

"Why ever not? La Casita is mine."

He observed her somberly. "It's yours all right. But the cottage is remote—for a woman living alone, that is." He reached out a hand and smoothed back a heavy strand of blonde hair. He looked at her, slowly and deliberately, with his blue eyes moving disturbingly from her bare feet up the slender legs, studying the gently curving hips, the flat stomach and small waist, fastening his gaze on the breasts swelling softly under the scant bodice of the black bikini, and resting at last on hair the color of pale honey. "A very lovely woman—alone."

She stiffened. "That's the way I like it. Alone."

He told her, "So there are two of us then." He turned away. "Just remember to keep your doors locked. All the time. It's not safe to be too trusting."

She said musingly, "There appear to be quite a few things around here that are dangerous. For me, that is."

He caught her by the shoulders with unexpected force. "Explain."

Ariana broke loose and stood rubbing the soft flesh of her upper arms. "Well, you tell me I shouldn't swim alone, and also that I'm to lock up at night, and—"

"And?" The dark blue gaze bored into her.

She shrugged, outraged. "I'll have bruises all over my shoulders tomorrow. Surely you know your own brute strength."

She watched him relax a little. "And that's all?" he asked curtly.

Gritting her teeth, she snapped, "It's enough."

He warned her softly: "See that you remember. I might not be around to haul you in next time. It's reasonably safe to swim near the shore, just stay away from that small reef. Shark and barracuda are attracted there by the little reef fish. Understand?"

She certainly did. He saw her shudder. "Look," he said, hesitating a little, "I'm sure I could help you get a job in Miami, a good job, an apartment too, perhaps. I think you'd be happier down there . . . plenty of young people, lots of potential dates—"

She was really angry now. "I've only just arrived and

you're trying to get rid of me. Why?" she protested. "What are you afraid of?"

His eyes narrowed, but she rattled on, ignoring the danger signals. "I'm going to stay, and if you think it's because I find you fascinating, Mr. Farleigh, well, think again. I've had enough of men to last my lifetime." Her head tilted back defiantly.

Dark eyes regarded her enigmatically. Then, swiftly, he pulled her into his arms and his mouth caught her lips, covering them, forcing them apart in a kiss that brought blood pounding in her ears, a kiss that penetrated deeper and deeper until she sagged against him. "Seb," she gasped, opening her eyes. "Seb?"

Dazed, he raised his head, and she saw the surprised look that touched his face for a moment before his mouth came down to her again with gentle kisses that brushed her lips, touched her cheeks, and kissed her brown eyes closed. When he spoke into the silence that pooled around them, his voice was harsh. "Chalk up another safety hazard for yourself," he said jerkily.

She leaned against the doorway. "So now there really are three? The sharks, and whatever it is that I am to lock out at night, and you, Seb?"

Afternoon sunshine shone on his face, shadowing the blue eyes, highlighting the dark hair. He reached out and touched her cheek, his fingers lingering in a brief caress. "Not I, Ariana," he said.

Sudden color stained her cheeks. He smiled at that and said wryly, "This has been *some* day . . . Best have an early night. I'll see you tomorrow."

*

She was tired when she got back from Delray late that afternoon with a car full of groceries and things like window cleaner and a new broom and a squeegee mop for the kitchen floor. And new shelf paper for the kitchen cabinets. There'd be other things she would need, she knew that, but she'd find them out as she went along.

While she made a cheese sandwich for her supper and boiled water for tea, her thoughts went winging back to Colorado. She missed her friends. If the phone company installed her telephone tomorrow, she'd call Lucy and tell her she was settled in and everything was okay. And it was, she thought. It really was. She had this darling cottage right on the ocean, and next week she would be looking for a job. You'd be proud of me, she'd tell Lucy and Emma, I'm getting right into the swing of things.

She took the teacup outside with her while she walked around the little cottage and inspected scarlet and yellow and white hibiscus and found some overgrown rose bushes. She thought the coral-flowered vine running up the outside of her bedroom wall was beautiful, and that the flowering white pinwheels were probably some kind of fragrant jasmine. On the south side there was a small, flagstoned patio with a yellow-tiled table and benches, surrounded by thick, protective vegetation, and a little sundial that said it counted only sunny hours. She could sit out there and write letters, and in no time at all her hands would be tan, a smooth golden brown, and the mark left by Ron's ring would disappear.

Clutching the cup, she stared moodily out to sea. The daytime breeze had almost died away, and the fronds of the coconut palms stirred sluggishly in the August warmth. As she watched, the sun sank beneath the western horizon and daylight drained away, darkening to the soft velvet of a tropical night. Overhead were the first stars.

Inside again, she rinsed out her cup and put the untouched cheese sandwich, carefully wrapped in a plastic sandwich bag, in the refrigerator. Perhaps she'd be hungry later. She leaned against the refrigerator for a moment. Something had flashed into her mind and then out again, leaving a fuzzy impression behind that eluded her completely as she tried to remember what it was.

She shrugged pretty shoulders. If it was something important, she'd think of it again. Meanwhile, she was going to change the shelf paper in the kitchen. If she stayed up late enough, surely she'd be so tired that she'd sleep as soon as she went to bed.

And not lie awake thinking of Ron.

It was getting better, she knew that. In a way Ron was just a memory. Time was on the wing, but sometimes she woke up in the still of the night with her face all wet with tears, and the old, familiar ache in her heart.

The new shelf paper was white with little yellow scallops, and first of all she fixed the shelves for the glassware, eight of everything in the exquisite Thistle pattern of Edinburgh Crystal—the dainty liqueurs and sherrys, clarets, white wines and saucer champagnes, the tall fluted champagnes, footed water goblets, and two large brandy snifters. She handled the crystal carefully, with genuine respect for the hand-blown pieces.

It was while Ariana was doing the shelves for the Coalport dinner service that she found the note tucked inside the covered Ming Rose sugar bowl. A letter from her great-aunt . . .

"Dearest Ariana," it began, and she scrambled down from the kitchen chair she had been standing on and curled up on the sofa by the fireplace to read it.

"I've just placed the last of my things in the cupboards. Cherished possessions, Ariana, and all for you. The Tiffany flat-ware is the Faneuil pattern, always one of my favorite sets, and the Coalport china was mine before I married. Enjoy using them just as much as I did, dear. Cecil and I bought the crystal on one happy trip to Edinburgh, and the seashell mirror in your bedroom has delighted me for many years. Meg and Luke have promised to keep an eye on things here until the time they are indeed all yours.

"The cottage is for you. That has been my intention

since Cecil died, Ariana. At that time I inherited the Court and all of its furnishings. But the Court is so very much a *Farleigh* place that after much thought I decided it should go back to my husband's people, specifically to his nephew Sebastian, whom Cecil loved as a son. Seb will be able to keep up the Court as it should be kept, and love it as it has always been loved. It would be too great a financial burden for you, my dear grand-niece.

"The British properties, of course, are mine only for my lifetime and revert to Cecil's people at the time of my death. And that is not long off now. God has been kind and given me the strength to do this thing I wanted to do for someone I have always loved dearly. You, my dear Ariana. Because every woman at some time in her life needs a bolthole—someplace to run to, to rest in, to love—a place where she can pause and refresh herself, I have arranged that La Casita is for you, on its own half acre of land.

"It is not to be sold or rented, and it is to be yours alone. Meg has helped me this last month, and we both think it is a lovely place again. Some years ago, when Cecil provided Meg and Luke with their own self-contained apartment within the Court—much like my own there, in fact—they moved from the cottage and it was used mainly for storage from then until now.

"I regret that you and I did not see more of each other, but we each have had our own responsibilities. Medical reasons have kept me much in England of late. First for Cecil's sake, and then with problems of my own. Bless you, my dear. May you spend many happy times here in La Casita, and may it be a comfort to you all the days of your life.

Lovingly, Margaret."

The letter was dated just five weeks before her death in England almost two years ago. Ariana wiped tears from her eyes and quietly reread the letter. She had been wrong earlier. It was more than material things that remained behind. Love remained, and kindnesses, and

many memories. She looked down at her hands and
blinked away new tears that threatened to spill down her
cheeks.

So Seb was to love and cherish the old Court as Cecil
had done? A good thing Margaret could not see the sheet-
shrouded furniture, the neglected gardens. Again that
little elusive thread of a thought shot through her mind
and then escaped as she tried to grasp it.

She stayed up late that night, working in the kitchen
until all the cupboard shelves were sparkling clean, and
wondered a little if Seb would see her lights and come to
see if all was well. At midnight she checked the locks,
turned out the lights, and climbed into bed.

Unfamiliar sounds kept her wakeful awhile. She was
just dropping off to sleep at last when she thought she
heard the throb of a motorboat, coming out of the inlet
and heading out to sea. And that was silly, she realized, for
who would be taking a boat out this late at night? She lay
listening for a few minutes, straining to hear, and then
punched up her pillow more comfortably and fell asleep.

Almost out of sight of land now, the 23-foot Seacraft
turned southwest in the direction of the Florida Keys, her
outboards at full throttle, moving over the midnight
water at a speed in excess of sixty miles per hour.

*

In the early morning hours before dawn touched the
sky, Ariana awoke with a start and sat up in bed, her heart
pounding. Again she heard the pulsing of a motor, more
muted now as it came in close to shore, dying away as the
boat sought and found safe harbor.

In the instant that the throbbing of the motors ceased,
Ariana realized how hungry she was. She hopped out of
bed and padded into the kitchen. There she poured herself a glass of cold milk, retrieved the cheese sandwich,
placed everything on a tray, caught up a napkin, and
returned to her bedroom.

Sitting up in bed with the tray on her lap, she ate the sandwich, chewing thoughtfully. Seb didn't want her to stay on at La Casita, that much she felt certain of. For whatever reason . . . Unhappily, she admitted that it was one more rejection, and it didn't do much for her confidence in herself. And since Colorado she badly needed confidence.

She glared down at her sandwich. All that talk of sharks and locking her doors! And then he had tried to tempt her to leave with the offer of help in getting a good job, even an apartment . . . but all of it way down in Miami, fifty miles away. A safe distance, she thought grimly. Too far to commute, especially in these days of high gas prices.

The milk was delicious. She drank the last of it, polished off the rest of the sandwich, and admitted that she herself had offered Seb the best weapon to get her out of there, handed it to him right on a silver platter when she'd told him that she had had enough of men to last a lifetime.

He'd used the weapon, too. Hot-cheeked, she recalled the ruthless kisses. *Of course.* Frighten the girl away with sexual advances, scare her off the premises. So far it was as easy to figure out as reading a book. She wriggled uncomfortably. It was what came next that puzzled her, that didn't fit the pattern, the moment when his lips had touched her face with gentleness, when his hand had caressed her cheek with a loving gesture. It wasn't part of what he had planned at all, whatever that might be.

She flicked off the bedroom lamp and used her new flashlight to find her way to the bathroom and then back to bed, to lie there, thinking.

Like it or not, she was forced to admit that Ariana Radnor as a permanent resident at the cottage seemed to be anathema in Sebastian Farleigh's eyes. But it was foolish to lose sleep over it, she decided. Heaven knows there was plenty of space around them here, so much that they need never cross paths at all if they didn't want to. And that would suit her just fine! Tomorrow—no, today—she'd tell him that.

It still puzzled her, though. The Farleighs were a wealthy family certainly, but she'd never thought of Seb as being a snob. And snob he surely was if he didn't want her around because she worked for a living.

However, Seb—if he *was* Seb, and of course he was for who else could he be?—had certainly changed a lot in sixteen years.

CHAPTER 4

"I'm glad someone thinks it's funny!" Ariana looked un-happily at the rain pounding down on her freshly painted bench. Outraged, she slammed the wet brush down on top of the still-open can of white enamel. Droplets flew and one landed straight on her rather pretty nose. Seb's laughter was the insult to the injury.

His mouth twitched. She was such a small fury, standing there soaking wet in white shorts and a striped tank top, with rain pelting down on them both. "It's just common sense not to paint in August, at least not in the afternoons when storm clouds mass in the southwest. This is rainy season in South Florida."

She sputtered, "I'm new here, remember? How was I to know? The sun was out bright as bright when I started."

He pushed the dutch door of the cottage ajar. "And it will be out again in twenty minutes or less. These showers are usually over soon." He indicated the open door. "Could we step in out of the rain, lady?"

Ariana touched her nose and the paint smudge smeared. "It's more like a deluge. I feel like Noah's wife."

They stood dripping on the kitchen floor, eyeing each other warily. "Are you cold?" she asked. "I can't very well lend you another shirt, but I'll get you a towel."

He shrugged. "I'm used to it." He peeled off the damp T-shirt and draped it over a broad shoulder. "You get in and change. I'll fix coffee while you get those wet clothes off. You did invite me in for coffee, didn't you?" His glance traveled deliberately over her, and she crossed her arms across her breasts in a protecting sort of gesture and looked away.

She was shy, he thought, this young girl. "Incidentally," he called after her, "put on pants and a long-sleeved shirt this time. You're getting too much sun."

He watched her stiffen, then march resolutely off to the bedroom. Whistling nonchalantly, he found the can of ground coffee, filled the small percolator with water and placed it on the electric range. His face sobered and he crossed the living room to look out to sea, his thumbs tucked in the waistband of his ragged blue denim shorts.

Ariana shut her bedroom door with a little bang and examined her face in the seashell mirror. The paint on her nose made her look like a clown, she thought, rubbing at it unsuccessfully with a towel. The good smell of coffee perking drifted in. Seb was making himself at home.

Deliberately, she donned a white bikini, reached for fresh shorts and a clean sleeveless blouse, dressed quickly, and wrapped a towel around her head before she returned, barefooted, to the kitchen. "Here's a towel, Seb. At least rub your hair dry."

He had the coffee poured and waiting for her, and had wiped off the wet vinyl tiles in the kitchen. "You're a quick changer," he remarked, looking her over. His eyes narrowed a bit at the blouse and shorts, and she waited for him to say something about that, but he did not.

"I've had a lot of practice." It was pleasant to have Seb in a good mood like this, but she was curious. "What did you want to see me about?"

His smile was silky. "Couldn't it be that I'm just being neighborly?"

She considered that for a moment. "I don't know," she told him honestly. "I've had the distinct impression all week that you thought my being here was a problem." She watched his face when she said that, and she thought she saw a flicker of something—alarm? regret?—touch those dark eyes.

"As a matter of fact," she added, "I've been waiting for a good opportunity to tell you this: that the farthest thing from my mind is being a burden to you, or taking advantage in any way of the fact that a great-aunt of mine was once married to your uncle, or—or anything."

His voice was abrupt. "And what the devil does all that mean?" He put his coffee cup down on the end table beside him and came to stand before her where she sat, her feet tucked under her, on the sofa. "Especially the 'or anything.'"

Her laughter was a little shaky. "Just that. Anything. I read my horoscope in yesterday's paper," she told him. "And it said this was my lucky week. Some luck! The first thing I try to paint gets all waterlogged."

His mouth thinned. He could be cruel, she thought then, really cruel. The Seb she had known long ago had been a kind, laughing person.

"Don't change the subject," he ordered, and his voice had a bite in it. "You were saying earlier that you didn't sleep well here. What's bothered you?"

She pulled the towel off and shook back her thick light hair. It was almost dry. "What did you say, Seb?"

"Quit stalling. I asked you what bothered you in the night." He sat down beside her, his long legs extending out on the green carpeting.

Leaning forward, she drank the last of her coffee. She decided that she would not mention the boat at all. "Oh, nothing—and everything," she answered. "I don't know, Seb, a combination of many things, I suppose."

He looked at her intently. "You're missing your friends," he said. "And that's apt to get worse, not better. What happened out there in Colorado to send you haring here for cover? Want to talk about it?"

"No."

A smile softened his rugged features. "You're not a woman to live alone, Ariana."

Her fingers began to tremble, and she thrust them behind her. She forced her voice to sound steady. "You have no idea what kind of woman I am, Seb. Besides, you live alone and seem to endure it rather well."

His smile was stiff. "A writer seeks quiet and solitude."

She reached across for his empty cup and carried them both back into the small, efficient kitchen. "Is that what you do—write?" she called back to him.

He was right behind her, right at her shoulder. "That's what I'm doing now." He asked her, "Why are you shouting?"

She had thought he was across the large living room, of course. Anyone would have realized that. "I didn't hear you—the carpeting—" She saw him glance at the clock. "Thank you for stopping over," she said politely. "I don't know yet why you came, but it did give me a chance to assure you that I'll be no bother to you, living here I mean. No bother whatsoever."

"I wonder." He touched the paint smear on her nose with one strong brown finger. "Turpentine," he said. "Or mineral spirits. And keep your eyes closed when you use it, hear me?"

"I'll do that," she promised hastily.

He said, "I'm glad the phone's finally in. You're not entirely isolated now. By the way, I came over to invite you to see a turtle hatching. Interested?"

She was rinsing the cups and turned around quickly, bumping into him in her eagerness. "Sea turtles? Near here?"

"Near here." He had one hand on the doorknob. "This rain will be bringing out another batch of them. I'll pick you up in the golf cart tomorrow afternoon about two. Wear sunglasses and a hat."

"I'll be waiting. And thank you, Seb."

He touched her arm. "You're a stubborn one. And don't

say I didn't warn you—you're getting too much sun. You'll make yourself ill."

*

Ariana scrambled an egg for her lunch, added celery stalks and an apple to her tray and poured a tall glass of iced tea, squeezing into it a generous slice of key lime from the tree near the dutch door. The rain had stopped and she inspected her paint job, upending the bench to let the water droplets run off. She decided it wasn't going to be too bad, after all. The quick-drying enamel had apparently already formed a protective skin.

She carried her tray out to the deck and ate her lunch watching a freighter half a mile off, steaming north with the Gulf Stream. Carrying what? she wondered idly, and decided that the cargo could be goods for northern markets, trans-shipped at Miami from boats that had come up from South America with coffee, minerals, fertilizers . . .

After lunch she read the classified ads in the newspaper that she had bought a day ago in Delray, taking a pencil and circling the advertisements that seemed to have possibilities. There weren't many. She chewed her lip thoughtfully and realized she was beginning to worry. And that was silly, because she'd only been there a few days and she had enough money to last at least a month without a job.

But after half an hour of culling, there were still only two circled ads that seemed to be even slightly worth considering. She put the paper aside, caught up her apple, and went down to the beach.

The view was beautiful—on one hand was the turquoise ocean as far as she could see, and off to her right, the waving fronds of palms and the silhouettes of the feathery casuarina trees. She walked along the water's edge, where the sand was firmly packed, and came soon to the wide inlet and the jetty that she had seen from the water a few days before.

Seb's property. Her eyes followed the green embankment and saw gardens and just one corner of a gray stone house with a tiled red roof. St. James Court.

The jetty had multiple moorings, and a channel had been cut from the inlet into the land alongside to make a water approach for boats. Rather large boats, too, she guessed, scrambling over the bridged walkway and down to the other side. She wondered how many boats would fit in the large stone boathouse built into the embankment. Besides the Seacraft, of course. Only one boat was moored to the jetty now, a smallish Boston Whaler, a pair of oars neatly stashed under the seats.

Once past the Court the beach was littered with seaweed from the last tide. There were seagrape bushes here, too, great tangles of them in the fringe of heavy shore vegetation, and a kind of cactus that she was surprised to see. Far above floated a few clouds, fluffy ones that seemed scarcely to move, and the gentlest of breezes blew to cool her warm face. Seabirds wheeled above, and everywhere, of course, were the beautiful palms.

Less than five minutes later she came upon a circular cove of crystal clear water bordered by powdery sand and a solitary cluster of thick palms that offered inviting shade. She cried out in pleasure. The sand held not a single footprint. The beach was all hers.

She stripped to her bikini and wandered in the shallow water, kicking up rainbow sprays of transparent drops, looking for shells. There were none, and she soon dropped down in the shade of the palms and burrowed her feet down to cooler sand, eating the apple.

She didn't remember relaxing, turning to lie flat on her stomach in the soft warm sand with her head pillowed on her outstretched arms and her hair flowing free . . . nor falling asleep while the earth's rotation seemed to move the sun across the sky. The wakeful hours of the previous night demanded payment, and Ariana closed her eyes and slept.

*

She awakened with the sun on her face and was immediately conscious of pain, the fiery pain of sun-scorched skin. Sand clung to her sticky body, and she was aware of great thirst. It hurt to move. She put out her hands and came slowly to a sitting position, then rose unsteadily to her feet.

Her head ached. She bent down with effort and retrieved her shorts and blouse, draping the white blouse over her head to shield her face from the golden sun. She was a little frightened at the way she felt, weak and nauseated. She was hardly ever ill, and this was something she had brought upon herself, sleeping in the sun for over one hour.

The ocean shimmered blue and invitingly cool, and she thought how good it would feel to lie down in the shallows and let the water wash over her burning body. However, she was afraid she'd never have the strength to get home at all unless she started now.

Each step was a separate chore. Her legs were stiff sticks, her body creaked. She plodded back along the beach in the direction of the cottage, moving slowly. Somewhere near the Court she thought she dropped her shorts. Nothing mattered now except getting home.

There, she sat on a kitchen chair and sipped cold water, trying to get the strength to walk to the bathroom. Finally she limped over and locked the dutch door, dropped her sand-encrusted swimsuit on the kitchen floor and made it to the shower.

Lukewarm water felt best. She let it flood gently through her long hair and over her aching body, cleansing away salt and sand and perspiration. It was useless to try to towel herself or dry her hair—her sunburned scalp hurt too much to touch, and even the soft terry of the bath towel rasped like a file against her scarlet back.

Whimpering a little, she found a cotton nightgown and

pulled it over her head, drank another glass of water, and was promptly sick to her stomach. She leaned over the basin, retching, then rinsed out her mouth and staggered to bed.

The ringing of the telephone awakened her from fitful sleep. She could not have gotten up to answer the phone even had she wanted to. She was cold now, shaking with a chill. Her teeth were chattering, and she slid painfully under the light blanket and pulled up the crocheted bedspread. And then she was too warm, frantic with warmth, and she fought her way out from the covers, wanting water to drink, wanting the phone to stop ringing—

The ringing ceased and the pounding on the door began. "Go away," she called, and her voice echoed strangely in her ears.

She heard nothing, not the key in the lock of the dutch door, nor the quick footsteps across the living room. "Ariana? Ariana, are you all right? Answer me, damn it!"

"Here," she called shakily. "Seb? Seb, I don't feel good."

There was the click of a light switch, and he stepped into her room. "My God," he said, bending low. "No wonder you feel ill." Cool hands touched her forehead. "Lie still—back in a minute."

She floated mistily in and out of sleep, and then he was back again, giving her pills to swallow, cutting the thin material of the gown so it slipped far down, and then carefully applying a soothing, medicated lotion to her burned back and shoulders, to the tender backs of her legs, spreading the cool cream with supple fingers that gently eased the pain.

"So good—" she sighed.

His mouth twisted and he shook his head. "You deserve a beating, letting yourself get burned like this. Can you sit up a minute? Here's something for you to drink."

He helped her turn over—slowly, carefully—and when she sat up her white nightdress slipped all the way down to her waist, and she clutched at the sheet and tried to pull it up across her breasts.

He smoothed her damp hair from her face and smiled at her. "It doesn't matter, but we'll put this around you if it will make you feel easier." He draped a soft shirt carefully around her burned shoulders. "Drink this," he said and held a glass to her lips.

The liquid was cool on her parched lips, cool in her dry mouth. It slid down her throat and she murmured her thanks.

"You'll sleep soon," Seb promised and eased her down again. She felt his hands spread the medication along her arms, down the front of her legs and over her thighs, around her neck and throat and on her poor sunburned face. There was a pause, and the coolness of the lotion came again, smoothed lightly over her young breasts.

He felt her tense, and his voice was matter-of-fact when he spoke, helping her turn over while he checked her back again. She heard a mutter of satisfaction, but the throbbing in her head had ceased and she wanted only to sleep.

She thought she was given a drink of water, and that he pulled up the sheet to cover her when she stretched out again on her stomach, but her eyes were closing . . . closing . . .

The man prowled the house, locking the french windows, turning off lamps and checking bolts. He waited an hour, then checked the girl again. She was sleeping with one hand up to pillow her cheek, breathing normally in quiet rest. He stood for several minutes, looking down at her.

Just after twelve. She'd probably sleep like that until morning. Yawning, he let himself out the dutch door, locking it behind him and pocketing the key, and strode off in the direction of the Court.

*

The next morning Ariana awoke near the usual time and reached stiffly for the Baby Ben on the table by her bed. Seven-fifteen. She flung back the sheet and saw that her nightgown was off her shoulders and bunched awkwardly around her waist. Memory stirred, flooded back. Sebastian Farleigh had been there in the night.

She sat on the edge of the bed and wriggled her shoulders experimentally. Still sore, but nothing like the evening before when she had felt on fire all over. The gown was neatly cut straight down the back for some eighteen inches, she discovered, remembering Seb's arrival with a healing lotion.

She had been an idiot, falling asleep in the sun like that. After being well warned, too. The puzzling thing was how Seb had known she'd needed help. And how had he gotten in?

A key, of course. His own key. To *her* door? She wasn't sure how she felt about that.

Her head still ached, but it wasn't too bad. The hairbrush, though, felt like a thousand little swords piercing her burned scalp and the comb wasn't much better. She stepped out of the ruined gown and finger-combed her hair into a semblance of order.

The soft white shirt that Sebastian had draped about her naked shoulders last night was flung over the rocker; she picked it up and put it on, and the much-washed cotton garment hung far down to her mid-thighs. No bra today; her sunburned skin could bear no straps, no pressure. Old shorts and the man's shirt would suffice. She turned up the cuffs on the sleeves in wide folds.

It surprised her to find that her feet were swollen. Her fingers, too. She peered into the seashell mirror and saw puffy eyelids.

"I'm a mess," she mourned.

"That you are," Seb agreed, and he was right there again, right in her bedroom. She was indignant, and opened her mouth to tell him what she thought of his coming in and out like that, free as you please, but he beat her to it. "I knocked," he said. "Three times."

And of course he'd come straight in then, for she might have still been ill. Like last night, or even worse.

"I'd like that key, please," she said, and he unhooked it from his key chain and dropped it in her shirt pocket—his shirt pocket—without a word of protest. "I brought breakfast," he told her, holding up a baker's bag. "Fresh sweet rolls."

He made coffee while she walked stiffly to the bathroom, and when she came out again he had the cherrywood table in the living room set for two with the Coalport dishes. Orange juice glistened in the Thistle clarets and a plate of warm Danish pastries shared center pride-of-place with a potted pink daisy from the fireplace hearth.

"You forgot the napkins," she said, bringing out paper ones. "I think I'm hungry."

"When did you eat last?" he asked, pulling out her chair.

She thought it had been lunch, yes, of course it had been lunch. "I had a scrambled egg and celery, and I ate an apple before I fell asleep on the beach."

"No breakfast?"

There had been no breakfast, and, of course, no dinner, but he was not supposed to be worrying about her, she reminded him. And at that he downed his orange juice and looked at her rather balefully.

"I'd like to think I could count on that," he said dryly. "Day one and I have to come in and close your windows; day two and I bring you in with a cramp; yesterday had you quite parboiled and thoroughly ill with it, too. What do you plan for the rest of your holiday, Ariana?"

She started to tell him it wasn't really a holiday at all, but he shot another question at her: "Ready to tell me yet what happened out in Colorado?"

She couldn't be certain whether he was serious or not,

and so she shrugged her sunburned shoulders, winced, and asked him, "Today's the day, isn't it? To see the turtles? What should I wear?"

He leaned back in his chair. "Enough to cover every inch of you. If you still want to go, that is."

Of course she wanted to go. She drank her orange juice, twisting the crystal stem to watch sunshine catch the facets, and missed his next question completely. "I beg your pardon, you said—?"

"I want to check your back."

A warm glow flushed her face. "No, I'm fine, truly I am. That lotion you used was really something." She looked shakily at him. "Leave the cream if you think I need more. I'll apply it myself after a shower."

"No shower—not for another few hours anyway. And if you're blistering, the turtle trip's off, understand?" He was standing now, glaring at her, and she glared right back. No man was going to dictate to her. Never ever again, not after Ron. She'd learned her lesson there.

He pulled her to him. "What a prickly little one it is. Lie down on the sofa, this will take only a minute."

Gently, he drew up the soft cotton of the old shirt. She winced, and then the lotion was spreading across her back, soothing, cooling.

"There," he said, wiping his hands, "that wasn't so bad, was it? You're fortunate. I thought the burn was going to be deep enough to blister. Apparently the salve was in time."

She heard herself ask, in a rather muffled voice because her face was down in the sofa cushions, "What time for the turtles?"

He helped her to her feet and scowled down at her so hard that she stammered, "What's the matter? What's wrong?" Were they back to the frigid hospitality of the first three days again?

"Not a thing," he answered, in a disinterested manner. "I'll come down for you about two. Be ready." At the door he looked back and reminded her curtly, "Long-sleeved shirt, slacks, hat, the works."

*

She was waiting by the bench, swathed from head to toes in sunproof coverings. Generous applications of zinc oxide coated her nose and cheekbones. A brimmed canvas tennis hat was pulled down firmly over her forehead.

"How do I look? Will I do?"

He inspected her slowly—white tennis shoes, white ankle socks, slacks, his old shirt with the sleeves rolled way down, sunglasses—"No gloves?"

Triumphantly, she whipped out a pair of white cotton ones all gussied up with ecru embroidery and blue french knots. He winced. "You'll do. How you look is quite another matter. Hop in."

She stole a sideward glance at him as the golf cart took them in the direction of the Court. He was wearing black swim trunks and sandals, and an unbuttoned tan shirt that disclosed a suntanned chest with short dark hair. He looked good, very masculine with those broad shoulders and that flat stomach and the crisp dark hair curling on his chest.

He looked cool, too, in the muggy heat of the August day. Ariana thought she had never been so warm before in her whole life. "You could unbutton the shirt," he suggested, "until we're out on the water." And when she shook her head emphatically, he laughed aloud.

"I'm all covered up," she admitted. "But there's nothing much underneath. Just me."

He asked, "Will you come to supper tonight? At the Court? Nothing fancy, for I'm doing the cooking, but I have a rather nice wine."

The long evenings alone were the hardest for her so far, of course, and it would be lovely to be with company tonight. Her life was going to be here, in Florida, and it was up to her to make friends soon or she'd be dreadfully lonely, but she had an idea that she and Sebastian Farleigh wouldn't travel much with the same people—ever. Right now, though, he was the only one she knew, and it was kind of him to offer.

"Thank you. Do we dress?" she asked lightly.

"You'll undress," he said. "I'll let you take the gloves and hat off when we dine—otherwise it's strictly come as you are."

He was laughing at her, but she didn't mind. He could laugh at her all he liked, just so he didn't get cold and withdrawn the way he did sometimes, making it hard for her to believe that the Seb she remembered and the silent, somber man were one and the same person.

They left the cart in the circular driveway before the Court and crossed the lawns to the stone staircase that led down to the inlet jetty. This was where Seb had carried her up to the house after the swimming incident, only now he reached for her hand and they went running down the steps. They were going in the Boston Whaler, and Seb helped her in and started the small motor. "We'll hug the shoreline," he explained. "Keep your eyes peeled for coralheads."

They turned south, moving slowly. Ariana saw the little cove and the cluster of palms under which she'd fallen asleep, and it reminded her. "Hey," she called out, getting his attention. "How did you know I might be needing help last night?"

He shouted back: "Saw you pass, heading home, and you were looking mighty weary. I gave you a few hours to rest up, then telephoned. You didn't answer, so I thought I'd better check."

"Lucky for me. Thank you, Seb, or have I said that before?"

He pointed off to the right. "We're going in there. We'll pull this craft right up on that sandy beach. Ready?" When they were a few feet off shore he cut the motor, jumped into the water, and guided the small boat in. Ariana waded in at his side.

All up and down, the beach seemed alive with a gentle stirring. They knelt in the sand and watched while all around them hundreds of tiny baby turtles hatched from multitudes of spherical white eggs laid in nests that were simply holes dug in the sand above the high tide line. One by one, the newborns began their sandy trek, instinctively flippering their way to the sea.

"The adult female green turtles leave the sea at night," Seb said, "and come ashore and dig their nests. Not all the females at once, you understand, but over a period of many days. They lay their eggs, sometimes as many as two hundred eggs in a single clutch, cover them with sand, and return to the sea."

Ariana was watching with awe one small hatchling that popped up almost beside them, stretching out its minute neck and turning blindly, unerringly, toward the ocean. "Poor wee thing," she crooned. "No turtle mothers to feed them and help them navigate across the beach, Seb? Not like ducks do? Or mother cats with kittens?"

"They're orphans, every last one of them, so far as parental guidance goes. They're on their own, even before they hatch out some two months after mama turtle lays her eggs. The sun is their only incubator."

Ariana was on her feet, stepping carefully, shepherding the tiny creature on its long crawl to the water's edge. She laughed delightedly as it tumbled in, turning over and over, then righting itself and swimming out of sight. "At least that one's home safe," she called back to Seb, who was picking up a baby turtle and examining it closely.

Hearing her, he pointed up to the gathering of wheeling, screeching seabirds above them. "Danger and death lurk everywhere. For the newborns that survive those greedy gulls, there'll be the hazard of sharks waiting for them just offshore. See how soft their shell is just after hatching, Ariana. It doesn't harden immediately, and that leaves them very open to attack by their various enemies, of which man is one, too."

She knelt beside him, their heads touching, and he let her feel the soft top shell. "That's called the carapace. Its bottom shell is the plastron." He turned the turtle over to show her, and the minute flippers flapped with alarm and the neck stretched out frantically.

Seb stroked the tiny head. "They have no teeth, turtles, but their jaws develop horny edges that can cut and slash quite effectively."

He replaced the hatchling on the sand again. She wanted to pick it up and help it reach the water, but Seb caught her hand and held it, and the baby turtle began its own long quest.

"We mortals interfere too much," Seb said, trying to place it all in perspective for her. "The crawl to the sea, the supper for the gull, the food for the shark—they're all part of nature and nature's cycle. Probably less than half of a sea turtle's eggs survive the weather and the predatory animals—and man is one of those, don't forget—and perhaps less than half of the hatchlings will ever live to become adults. So nature sees to it that hundreds and hundreds of eggs are laid. This beach is just one place of thousands throughout the tropical world where the green turtles come to make their nests, and this crowd we're seeing born today is just one batch. There were some born yesterday; there'll be more tomorrow."

She looked so anxious, her sunglasses pushed far up and the brown eyes troubled. He gave her fingers a comforting squeeze. "Glad you came?" he asked. "Even if the story isn't all sweetness and light?"

She had never seen anything quite like this turtle hatching in her life. The wonder of it caught at her heart. "I'm terribly grateful to you, Seb. I'd be so much the poorer for having missed this. Tell me, how did you know—about the hatching, I mean?"

He'd been cruising the shoreline the day before, looking for a piece of equipment that had floated off, and had seen the unusually heavy gathering of gulls. "A sure sign," Seb said. "And I thought it might interest a newcomer."

That sounded as if he was considering her as someone other than a three-week tourist, she thought happily. Newcomer was a word that meant more than "here today, leave tomorrow," didn't it? She beamed at him and mopped her sweaty face with a handkerchief.

Seb must have read her mind, for he frowned, his dark brows coming straight together and his eyes aloof again. "Let's get on home," he said coolly. "You've had enough sun for today, and I think you'll want to rest awhile before you come over for dinner."

CHAPTER 5

Seb was on the wide terrace, the one that looked seaward, doing something at a gas barbecue grill when she came walking slowly up the gravel drive. The blue gaze swept briefly over her. "Hello," he said. "You needn't have changed."

He had, though, into a blue silk shirt and impeccably tailored light trousers, and his skin was like bronze against the blue of the partly opened shirt. She thought, a little wonderingly, that he was probably the best-looking man she had ever seen, more handsome than Ron even, and that, she said to herself, was really something.

She was looking as good as she could with a massive dose of sunburn. After a cool shower she had decided to wear a long patio skirt, white cotton with rose- and lemon-colored flowers printed here and there, and a rose stretch tube top that just dropped down over her head and was pulled into place, because her sore back simply could not tolerate a bra yet, and Seb's old cotton shirt was soiled after the day's expedition to the turtle hatching.

Her brown eyes held an almost happy look, and the honey-blonde hair was brushed back and caught at the nape of her neck with a rose velvet ribbon.

"How are you on salads?" Seb asked, and she laughed and told him, "Middling. Is the dressing ready, or shall I start one from scratch?"

"From scratch." He'd been living alone for a month, he reminded her, and if his couple, Luke and Meg, weren't back soon he was going to have to advertise in "help wanted" for a cook. "And someone to tidy up the place," he added.

He was joking, of course, and so was she when she retorted, "Maybe I should apply. It would be convenient employment, and no waiting for the bus."

He asked warily, "You're still determined to find a job hereabouts?"

"Well, my financial situation isn't exactly very sound," she admitted. "Yes, of course I'm going to have to find work."

He asked, "Can you locate the kitchen without me? If you'd start the salad fixings, I'll stay here and tend the steak. Something's wrong with the grill, but I'll have it fixed in a few minutes."

He had stripped off the protective dust sheets from the furniture, she noticed as she walked through the large living room on her way to the other wing. It looked welcoming, lived in again, with lamps glowing against an early dusk and the table laid by the sliding glass doors so they would be able to see moonrise over the upper level gardens.

The kitchen was a friendly, efficient place. It had been updated recently, she decided, looking at modern cupboards of fine, waxed wood, a microwave oven, matching freezers and refrigerators, two of each of those two . . . She found tomatoes, lettuce, and large white mushrooms, everything rinsed and ready to use, and she washed her hands and got to work. A bottle of uncorked red wine, a Bordeaux-St.Émilion, waited on the wheeled butler's table. She sniffed it appreciatively as she passed.

Seb stuck his head around the corner. "Ten minutes," he warned. "Ready?"

She thought so. She watched him reach down wine glasses and scoop up a warming platter. "I didn't make drinks; I got busy tinkering with the grill, but we have a fine Bordeaux."

"Is everything set then?" she wanted to know, placing the salads on the wheeled cart. He added thickly cut, crusty bread, and took artichokes braised in butter from a warming oven. "You wheel in," he said. "I'll bring the steaks."

They ate at the table by the massive glass doors, while starshine and moonglow illumined the gardens, and off-shore an occasional freighter traced its way north with the Stream.

"What have you planned for tomorrow?" Seb asked pleasantly.

Ariana looked up from the last of the delicious meal. "Mmm—absolutely marvelous food. I was even hungrier than I thought," she admitted, with a half-embarrassed laugh that caught in her throat. "The steak was perfect, Seb."

He nodded that handsome head of his. "You still haven't told me about tomorrow, have you? Well, we'll let that go for a bit." He wagged a finger at her. "I'm old enough to give you some advice: don't fall into the habit of scratch meals, living alone. Unless you eat properly—fresh vegetables, fruit every day, enough protein for your body's needs—you'll pay the bill in lower resistance to disease and general poor health."

"Yes, doctor," she said, mockingly, and he reached out for her hand.

"Sure you're all right financially? For the essentials?"

From across the table she could sense the powerful attraction of this man. The cool strength of his hand comforted her, and in the soft glow of the lamps the dark gaze seemed to hold a sincere friendship. "Yes, I'm all right money-wise, for the time being, while I look for work. And that's what's on for tomorrow, Seb." She reminded him, "I'm what's known as a working girl, you know. From way back."

"Nothing wrong with that, so why sound defensive?" His hand released hers and he reached for the wine, poured a little more into her glass and added some to his own. The lamp glow shone ruby-red in the cut-glass design of the Waterford crystal as he turned it reflectively between long, lean fingers.

Almost shyly she watched his quiet face, wishing she understood his many moods better. "I found a letter from my great-aunt. She'd tucked it in the sugar bowl for me to find."

He raised dark eyebrows. "And?"

She was silent for a moment, and then spoke intensely. "I wish I'd seen more of her, Seb. I wish I'd known her better, once I grew up. Margaret was a wonderful person. She said the Court had to go back to you when she died, that that was not just fair, which it was, but that you'd be able to cherish it as they had done." Her voice was low, grave. "The hours she must have put in, she and Meg, making the cottage so liveable for me. Because every woman needed a bolthole, Margaret said, and she wanted La Casita to be mine. My bolthole. If I ever needed one."

The honey-blonde head drooped. He leaned over and trailed a finger just under her lower lashes. "Why are you crying?"

At that she sat straight up and announced indignantly, "I'm not crying." The lovely brown eyes brimmed over and, childlike, she dashed the tears away with her fist. Seb silently passed her a clean white handkerchief and she dried her eyes and admitted, "Well, only a little. I was suddenly so lonely for—for everything that's gone." She laughed a little shakily and said, "Perhaps it's the wine, making me all weepy and sentimental. This stretch top is hurting me, too."

The moon was flooding the gardens with pale, pale light, and faint perfume from white ginger or star jasmine touched her nostrils. The evening breeze came, fresh and sweet, smelling of ocean. She murmured, "It's so beautiful, Seb—the calm and peace of a tropic night."

He had come up behind her, taking her by the shoulders to turn her to him, and she cried out in pain and broke away. She heard him catch his breath. "My God, I forgot your sunburn," he exclaimed, taking her hand and steering her gently to a double lounger on the terrace. "Wait here," he said, "I'll get more lotion."

She caught at his hand. "No, please stay. The pain is gone."

At that, he eased his long length to the lounger beside her. "You're sure?"

"Quite sure." It wasn't, of course; the elastic in the tube top was much too tight, but she didn't want him to leave, she didn't want this peaceful time between them to end.

"Tell me about him," Seb said, his voice as quiet as the night about them.

Ariana watched the moon race a small bank of clouds. "Him?"

"The one you're running from, the one in Colorado. Did you love him?"

He was looking at the moon, and not at her at all, and somehow that made it easier for her to speak. "What does that matter now? It's all over. His name was Ron, Ron McLinn. We—we were engaged to be married."

He was patient, not rushing her to talk. "Colorado is a long way away," he said.

"Yes, a long way . . . I was assistant social director at Montval—that's the old, very elegant all-year resort near Denver, you know—and Ron was assistant manager there. We met, fell in love, and then he met someone else, someone with nine million dollars." Her voice trembled. "End of story."

He challenged, "You mean you just sat back and let Miss Manybucks take over? You gave him up, just like that?"

"No, not really. It was all over anyway, don't you understand?"

"Well, then?"

Her voice had dropped almost to a whisper. "Everything seemed to happen to me about then. I began to make mistakes—in my job, I mean. Rather bad errors. I mixed up some dates, and then I forgot an important appointment. Well, I didn't forget it exactly, I just thought it was at another time, nine instead of five. And one night I set up a dinner party, to honor someone's birthday, and I got the numbers wrong, fifty instead of fifteen, and that was a shame for I adored old Mrs. Barton and I wouldn't have hurt her feelings for anything.

"But my worst goof was scheduling a rather large convention." Her voice was wobbling now, and Seb reached out and took her hand. "I tentatively booked them in on dates that were already taken—in December rather than September. Emma French, she was my boss, was supposed to fire me, but instead I was sent to see a Denver physician. I guess they thought I was having a nervous breakdown. Because of Ron, you know—"

Her voice trailed away, and Seb looked at her. "And was that why?"

"No," she continued softly. "Oh, I don't know. Maybe it was. But I considered myself a professional, you see, so I thought it had to be more than—than Ron and me. It had started before we actually broke up, maybe about the time I first suspected something about him and Mrs. Fayette, so perhaps they were right. I don't know."

He asked, "What did the Denver man say?"

She blinked away fresh tears. "He—he said something about being in jobs one couldn't handle and subconsciously trying all kinds of angles to get out."

"Was that all he said?" Seb sounded angry.

"Well, that was mainly it. And on my way home from seeing him I had an accident. Not in the car, just after I had left it. I was late for an appointment to go riding and that worried me, and I guess I was in too much of a rush to look out for cars. A taxi ran into me, or rather, I ran into it. I wasn't badly injured, just knocked about a bit, and when I was feeling well again, Emma French—she's a love—got me a three-month sick leave."

"And what about Ron?"

"Oh—well—there were still those nine million dollars, weren't there?"

"So you ran for your bolthole," he said slowly.

She sniffed and nodded, and he passed her the handkerchief again. "I've stayed at Montval," he said. "You must have been good to get the job you did at a place like that. You can type?"

"Type, and some shorthand, and all the usual graces," she laughed, a bit shakily. "I was good at it. At least until everything seemed to fall apart at once."

"You're probably exaggerating what happened. Just wait, some big hotel will snap you up," he assured her. "Just the name *Montval* and they'll be lining up, wanting to hire you."

"No. I've lost confidence in myself, Seb. I feel—inadequate. After all my goofs, and then Ron—yes, and after that Denver doctor, too—I wouldn't dare try for something with real responsibility again." She shook her head, and a strand of her hair drifted across his cheek. She reached out a hand to retrieve it, and Seb pulled her into his arms.

The pain of it caught in her throat. "What is it?" he demanded.

"It's this stretch top," she stammered. "I wore it because I couldn't stand a bra on my sore back yet, but this wasn't a good idea either, I'm afraid. The elastic threads are catching little folds of my sunburned skin. Seb, please —have you another old shirt, a soft one? I can't stand this much longer."

"Now," he said, "I've heard of everything in the way of excuses."

Her lips opened wide in a gasp of protest, and Seb lowered his dark head to hers and kissed her mouth, trailed kisses on her cheeks, and, gently, on her poor shoulders. Their lips touched, clung. Their bodies quivered and drew closer. When he took his arms away, she felt bereft.

His voice was husky. "I'd better get that shirt."

The telephone shrilled as he was crossing the living room on his way back to her, and she saw his frown. He passed her the shirt and took the call, watching her as she stood up in the moonlight and turned her back to him and shed the stretch top. The shirt felt cool on her burned skin, and she buttoned it up, hearing his voice saying things like: "No, not yet . . . I don't want to handle it that way . . . that's impossible at this time . . . I'll inquire . . . only if there is no other way . . . same time, then—"

His hands were gentle on her face when he came to her again. "Better?" he asked, and she said yes, but that it was time for her to go home. He hesitated only a moment and then told her: "I've been waiting for that call. Attorney friends of mine in Coral Gables. There's a job there for you with them, if you'd like—receptionist and some typing. Nothing too rigorous. And by a lucky coincidence, they know of an apartment for you, too. Near the main campus of the University of Miami, only four blocks from their office building. A sublease arrangement, the rent's reasonable because the owner insists on a responsible party."

"Someone like me."

"Exactly. This could be what you're looking for, Ariana. You could laze around here another ten days or so and then start work right after Labor Day."

She doubted it. It was just too much of a coincidence. All her newfound confidence in Seb was going up in smoke. "Well, I'll think about it," she said. "Thank you, of course, but it's probably too far away for me. Coral Gables is right next door to Miami, isn't it?"

He said firmly, "I think you should grab it—the position and the apartment. Why don't we ring them back and say you'll start September second?"

She walked right past him to the side entrance and said politely, "Goodnight, and thank you. Dinner was delicious, and I had a lovely time with you tonight."

"I'm running you back," he said coolly, his lips tight, and she thought how strange it was that that same mouth had kissed her only minutes before, and his lips had been warm and tender.

"Are you asking me in for coffee?" he inquired when the golf cart rolled up to the dutch door. He extended his hand for her key and she held the little flashlight so he could see the lock.

"Not tonight," she said, and put out her hand for the key.

"You should leave some lamps on when you go out in the evening," he reminded her, turning back to the cart.

"I did. One lamp. It's out, though. The bulb must have been old."

He came back then and wanted to see her safely in. "I'll check the place over for you," he offered.

"Thank you, no." She'd heard *that* line before. "Goodnight again."

When he said, "See you tomorrow then," she just waved. It wasn't until she'd gone in, though, locked the door behind her and switched on some lights, that she heard the sound of the golf cart starting up the path to the gravel drive back to the Court.

The first thing she noticed was that one of the french doors to the deck was ajar. Ariana closed it firmly, shot the bolt, and went off to the bedroom to get ready for bed. Seb would have given her a rocket if he'd seen that! She really was going to have to be more careful.

She crossed the green carpeting, pulling the ribbon from her hair, and decided to replace the burned-out bulb in the end table lamp. Next time, she thought, she'd leave two lamps burning. Just to be sure. But the old bulb was warm to the touch, and, puzzled, she turned on the lamp.

Light pooled around her. The old bulb was definitely not burned out at all.

If she was going to make a success of living alone, she couldn't fly off in a tizzy any time something happened to startle her. She knew that, but her heart was pounding and she felt uneasy. There could be all sorts of explanations for the business with the lamp, like maybe that wasn't the one she'd left on, after all. Or perhaps there'd been a surge in the electric current while she was out, and the bulb hadn't been able to take it.

And it could be just a coincidence that the french door had been ajar . . .

Her thoughts in a turmoil, Ariana went from room to room, checking. Tomorrow, she decided, she'd call a locksmith from Delray to come out and change the locks, all of them, right through the whole house. She should have thought of that earlier. It was a sensible precaution, especially for a woman living alone.

Nothing seemed to be missing, she decided. Nothing was stolen. Everything was just as she had left it, so there probably hadn't been anyone in at all. It was just her own forgetfulness about the lamp. And about the french door.

Although—She sat down on the end of her bed and studied her dresser top. Something—she couldn't be quite certain what—seemed different about the placement of things. Her brush and comb and hand mirror. It was the brush, she decided. She hadn't left it there at all.

Or had she?

No, she had not. She was certain of that now. She recalled how she had brushed her hair, gingerly, very very gingerly because her scalp still hurt from the sunburn, and she'd been standing out on the deck, watching the ocean. She'd left the brush there, on the little deck table, when she'd gone to fetch the ribbon. But what possible interest could her hairbrush have to anyone?

Outside, a night bird called, and the darkness seemed waiting . . . sinister. She felt the first twinge of fear.

Her fingers were shaking as she caught up the telephone and dialed. Seb answered on the second ring. "Please come," she begged. "Someone has been in the house and I'm frightened."

"I'm on the way," he told her and she heard the instrument slam down into place.

When footsteps pounded up the path, she raced to the door and threw it wide, flinging herself into his arms. The contact with his body brought an instant feeling of safety. His arms enfolded her. His voice warned, "Don't you ever check before you open your doors? I could have been a complete stranger."

"I'm sorry," she gasped. "I was scared."

He put her gently from him. "Let's take a look around."

She clung to his sleeve as they walked around the cottage. Seb inspected the bolt on the french doors, listened while she babbled on about warm light bulbs and a hairbrush.

He was astounded. "And that's all?" he asked her. "Just these insignificant things and you're convinced someone's been inside?"

A chill ran down her spine. Seb thought it was her imagination gone wild, but she knew that while she had been to dinner at the Court someone had been moving about in her cottage, touching her things. She said quietly, "You don't believe me, do you? But it's true. I felt uneasy as soon as I came in, there was a sort of waiting feeling." Waiting for something to happen, she meant.

They made a full tour of the place, and then walked together around the outside while Seb looked at window fastenings and checked the beach below the cypress deck. They went back to the parking lot and her rental car was there, locked, undisturbed.

"Make some coffee," he suggested when they came back in. "There's got to be an explanation. I've just had an idea and I want to check it out."

She watched him from the kitchen counter while he

used her telephone. Eight digits, she counted, measuring out instant coffee into two buttercup-yellow mugs. Eight digits meant a long distance call, didn't it? Someplace within the same area code, but not local—

The phone rang quite a while before the party at the other end picked it up. Fascinated, Ariana watched tension build up in Seb's face. The lines there deepened; fingers tapped impatiently. She had his coffee ready by the time he began to speak, and she brought in the mug and placed it on the hearth where he could reach down easily and get it.

His questions were crisp. She couldn't help hearing some of it, although she purposely went back into the kitchen and busied herself, nervously fixing her own cup of coffee and a plate of cookies for Seb.

"You'll never believe this," he said to her at last, bending down for a quick sip of the hot liquid. "Never in ten thousand years."

She was huddled on the sofa, a dismal little bundle of cotton nightgown and hastily donned robe. "Tell me quickly."

"Well, it really solves the whole thing," he said, coming over to scoop her up in his arms and sit back in the big lounge chair with her on his lap. "Listen," he said. "It was an old friend of mine, an old army buddy who used to doss down here whenever he came through town late at night. We let him have a key; there wasn't anything in here in those days except stored lawn furniture, some cots, stuff like that, you know, and he's a pilot with a miserable schedule—lots of night flights. He said he cleared out fast when he saw the place had changed, female frippery all over the bedroom."

Seb's hands were stroking her hair, gently because he remembered about the sunburn. "Bunte wouldn't hurt a soul. Feel better about it now?" he asked lightly.

She did. Immensely so. "How did you happen to think of him if he hasn't been through here for awhile?" she asked, relaxing a little now, enjoying his nearness, her earlier thoughts about the job near Miami quite forgotten.

He pulled her closer, his hands lightly touching her shoulders, and the robe slipped away, and then the cotton gown. His fingers traced a line down over her chin to her throat, down the lovely arch of her neck to the little hollow between her breasts. "Ariana?" His voice held the unspoken question.

All of her was responding to him, responding with thudding heart and trembling body. "Wait—" she stammered. "Answer me first, Seb."

His gaze slid to her mouth, and then he was kissing her, tasting her lips, covering them with his own while his hands possessively explored her body. He said huskily, "I've forgotten what you asked. I've forgotten everything except that we're two lonely people who seem to have found each other." He stroked her hair, her satin cheeks, the soft skin of her neck, and then his mouth came down upon hers again, seeking the sweetness of her in a deep embrace.

"You're beautiful," he said, and his voice was suddenly harsh. "Very beautiful." He carried her to her bed and laid her gently down. "Don't be frightened. Don't ever be afraid of me. I'd never harm you."

She gazed wordlessly at him, and he came to lie beside her for a moment, holding her quietly. "Think you can sleep now?" he asked huskily, raising himself to look down at her. "If I don't leave now, darling, I'll never leave. Goodnight—we'll talk tomorrow. Just don't worry anymore, you're safe. Quite safe." He touched her eyes with his lips, closing them. "Go to sleep. I'll lock up and let myself out."

*

She woke in the night, coming suddenly wide awake and propping herself up on one elbow. The bedside clock said almost two. She was aware of noise, the dull throbbing pulse of a powerful motor.

That boat again. And nearby. She lifted her head, straining to hear.

Often, weeks later, she wondered why she hadn't just reached for her bedroom telephone extension and dialed Seb. It would have been so natural a thing to do—to telephone and say, "Look, I'm sorry to keep disturbing your sleep, but there's some big boat that's running near your channel, and I sort of wondered—"

Something stayed her hand.

She settled back against the pillows and closed her eyes, but a thought in her subconscious darted in and out of her mind, never quite surfacing, keeping her wakeful. It had something to do with what had been said that night . . . or was it something about the cottage?

There—she had it! She opened her eyes and stared at the ceiling. Seb's friend Bunte—If Aunt Margaret had fixed up the cottage for Ariana the last few months of her life, and Ariana knew that she had done just that, then Bunte certainly hadn't stopped by here for at least two years or he would have known about the changes. Seb had as much as said that Bunte only occasionally stopped at the cottage *back when it was used as a storage spot.* And it hadn't been used that way for two years. Yet Seb had gone straight to the phone and dialed this man, not checking the phone number in the directory, not asking help of the operator. Pretty good memory, she decided. Too good . . .

In fact the whole thing about Bunte was a little weak when you examined it, she decided. Examined it thoughtfully and not all distracted by kisses, that is. It wasn't likely, for example, that a person would blithely unlock the door of a place he didn't own, certainly not after an absence of two years. He'd apparently arrived tonight in the early evening hours, and it would have been only reasonable for him to simply stop off at the Court and ask someone there if everything was still okay for him to stay over in the cottage.

Her brown eyes no longer drooped with sleep now. She lay still, putting the puzzle together. This "Bunte" was only part of the puzzle, a late part, at that. It had really all begun, she knew, when she had arrived at La Casita six days ago.

Seb must have been expecting her. After all, the attorney had been in touch with him, and then her lawyer's secretary had brought out the groceries to get her started. And Seb had added the wine. He'd said that first night that they'd been awaiting her arrival. Probably he thought she was taking a two-week vacation, seeing her new property, and then flying back to Colorado again, for he'd known that she worked at Montval. He knew, too, that she had originally planned to rent the place because it was just too far away from where she lived to be of real use to herself.

Perhaps a friend of Seb's had been making free use of the cottage. Fixed all up as it was, it was a real attraction, certainly. And maybe Seb had forgotten to warn him— her?—away for the while she, the owner, was here. She considered that idea and abandoned it promptly, for Seb had at least six guest rooms in the Court, plus Aunt Margaret's former flat. There'd be no point in using a place that didn't even belong to him. Seb wasn't like that. At least, she didn't think that he was.

But he was certainly anxious to move her out, wasn't he? When he found out that she was planning to stay, he'd gotten friends to offer her a good job. *And* an apartment, and apartments were mighty few down that way. But job and apartment were far down the peninsula, not near the Court.

And there was something about that job and its accompanying place to live that was just too pat altogether. She put her hands behind her head and lay there wishing she dared put on a light, wishing that she had a cup of tea.

Everything seemed to come right back to Seb, she thought sadly. Whatever it was all about, apparently it would not have mattered much if she had planned to stay only two, three weeks or so. He'd even encouraged that. Stay and laze around a couple of weeks, he had said, and then grab up this job and start the first of the month. So it wasn't a brief visit here that bothered him, it was Ariana as a possible permanent resident in the cottage—or near the Court?—that created the problem.

Why? What on earth was it all about?

She gnawed at her bottom lip, thinking hard. Either something was going to happen around here, or might happen soon around here—something she was not supposed to see, not intended to become aware of—And it was something that could somehow be delayed or postponed for an interval of time, say as much as three weeks, but longer than that would bring complications.

She pondered what the "something" might be. The Farleighs were a very wealthy family, so whatever the problem was it couldn't have to do with money. At least, that didn't seem very likely to her. And then came the remembrance of Ron's eyes as he said "Nine million bucks!" and she realized she wasn't sure of anything anymore.

Way back, she thought she remembered that Sebastian had planned to study medicine, and she wondered what had happened to change his mind and make him a writer instead. She couldn't recall ever hearing about any book he had written. Wouldn't Aunt Margaret have mentioned it sometime, say on a Christmas card? She realized that all she really knew about Sebastian Farleigh was from sixteen years ago.

He had been—well, not rude exactly when she'd come this time, but certainly aloof. Definitely distant—at least most of the time. Her cheeks burned. His kisses had been just sham, nothing else at all, to distract her from seeing too much, from asking questions.

He'd been extremely adroit at avoiding questions, she remembered. That made her sad, for she had been attracted to him right from the start, almost ready to put Ron from her mind and begin living again. She thought forlornly of the good companion at the turtle hatching, and the way he'd come to help when her sunburn had been so bad, and of the gentle kisses that one time. All pretense?

In her heart she could not yet be certain. I don't understand him at all, she thought with a sigh.

She groped for the flashlight and padded out to the kitchen, making herself a cup of tea in the dark, using the flash only intermittently so that no one would see her light and come to check if she was asleep, or make certain that she hadn't heard the boat. For the mysterious boat that ran at night was part of the puzzle, she was certain of that much.

Yesterday at noon she had put the last of some graham crackers in a sandwich bag, and now she carried the little packet and the tea back to bed. She opened the shutters wide and sat up against the pillows, sipping tea in the dark and looking out on the moonlit ocean.

Her earlier sense of fear was all gone, replaced now by what was a kind of anger that had burned away her fright. She felt disappointment, too, and the challenge of a puzzle she could not understand.

She opened the plastic and munched on the crackers. Yesterday's newspaper, she recalled, had reported again on the large numbers of illegal aliens—Haitians, Cubans, Colombians—being smuggled daily into South Florida for as little as thirty dollars each and as much as a thousand dollars or more. The unscrupulous smugglers, who cared nothing for the law nor the lives of the people, dumped their "cargo" ashore at night, often making them swim the last mile. Many of the aliens drowned; most were found when daylight came, walking the Miami streets barefoot and hungry, knowing no English, ill and confused. The mysterious night boat made her think of that newspaper article again.

She smiled a little. She could see Seb, back a hundred years ago, smuggling brandy or silks out of France, past the government excise cutters, and into English cellars. But participate in the squalid traffic in bodies that plagued Florida now? No, that was definitely not Seb's style. Whatever Seb was doing with his boat at night, she was absolutely certain he would not involve himself in smuggling aliens.

So much for the boat theory—

The hands of the clock crept near three, and she drank the last of the tea. Next morning would be a dead loss if she didn't get some sleep soon. She'd already made up her mind to get an early start to Delray Beach to begin looking for a job. There were two employment agencies in Delray; she'd try them first.

She turned on her side, settling down under the sheet, and she heard the crackle of something near her arm. The cracker wrapper— She reached for it, rolled the small plastic bag into a little ball, and tossed it blindly in the direction of the waste basket.

And the next piece of the puzzle suddenly fell into place.

Empty plastic envelopes spilling out from a cardboard box, spilling out across the muted rose and beige and green of the Court's priceless silk Princess Bokhara rug . . . and Seb thrusting the box hastily out of her sight.

A little despairing sound escaped her throat. Drugs, of course. *Of course.* She turned on her pillow and wept, and the hurt of it reached way to her heart.

CHAPTER 6

The first thing that came into her mind as soon as she opened her eyes the next morning was the knowledge that she didn't want to see Seb. Not yet. Not until she'd had time to think this whole thing through again and decide what she was going to do about it.

If anything, she admitted drearily, showering and dressing rapidly in a crisp beige cotton that had her initials monogrammed in emerald. A beige purse and low-heeled emerald sandals completed the outfit.

She wasn't used to the humidity of a Florida summer yet, and she brushed her blonde hair into a high French twist to keep it off her nape. She looked cool and competent, she decided, viewing herself in the full-length mirror on the back of the bedroom door, and hoped her neat appearance would last when the temperature soared as the August day progressed.

In Delray Beach she parked the rental car in a municipal lot near the ocean and walked over to a park bench just on the edge of the sand. The bench sparkled with salt crystals in the early sunshine. Ariana dusted off a spot with a clean handkerchief and sat down, enjoying the relaxing atmosphere of a deserted beach with piping shore birds darting along the water's edge while pelicans dipped and soared, searching for breakfast.

She was hungry, too, and she found a coffee shop in a small hotel across the beach boulevard and ordered grapefruit juice, milk, and a toasted English muffin. Guava jelly was served with her breakfast, and she spread the amber-colored preserve on her muffin, enjoying the piquant tropical taste.

The first employment agency was in a dreary second-floor room, but the woman who motioned Ariana to a chair near her desk was friendly and helpful. "You're over-qualified for most of our openings," she admitted after they had talked for a while. "You'd be bored in a week." She riffled through her cards. "Night shift maid at the hospital—part-time driver for a nursing home—janitorial aide at our biggest department store—" She pulled one card and considered it for a minute. "This one would do. How'd you like to try for cruise director of entertainment on the SS *Smerelda?* It does those five-day trips out of Port Everglades near Miami."

Ariana said no. "I need to find work near here where I live."

"Live-in maid—tutor in Greek?—maid—maid—maid —couple to take full responsibility for all cooking and gardening—secretary needed—oh Lord, not him again!"

She extracted the card and made a face. "Secretary, indeed. He's a well-known businessman, but the girls we've sent him have needed to be nimble sprinters more than shorthand stars. If you know what I mean," she said to Ariana, marking the card with a red pencil. "I'm recommending male secretaries for him from now on." She looked up. "There's really nothing else today."

She saw Ariana's worried face and frowned. "Wait a minute, I've just thought of something." She reached for the telephone, dialed. "Hi, Sue? Elaine here. Remember telling me about that opening out at Paradise? Are they still looking for someone? I've got just the girl here. Real class. Oh—well, yes, I see. Have a nice day."

"They withdrew the job offer yesterday. Going to wait until October to hire, I guess. Things are slower in the summer around here. Paradise is one of our tourist attractions," she explained. "A real nice place—all pretty gardens and parrots.

"Look, why don't you try at Falcon's? They serve another level of employment. With your credentials, you're more likely to find something there."

Falcon's was all starched collar and top hat atmosphere. Governess to the three young children of a Portugal-based diplomat—executive secretary to a bank president —manager of exclusive flower shop in Palm Beach— "What kind of employment *are* you seeking then, Miss Radnor?" they asked. If these splendid Falcon openings don't interest, is what they meant. Falcon's recommended the nearest state employment agency and gave her directions for finding the place.

"I have an opening for a medical secretary," the interviewer there said, chewing on her pencil. "But you don't qualify for that. The truth of the matter, Miss Radnor," she said, slipping off her glasses to look more closely at Ariana, "is that you're just too qualified for many of our openings and not prepared at all for the others. But check with us again early next week, why don't you. We get new listings nearly every day." She wished Ariana good-bye and good luck. "We have your telephone number and we'll call if something turns up that sounds just right for you," she promised.

The prospect of doing the rounds of the department stores, one after the other, checking for employment at their various personnel offices, was a daunting thought. Ariana felt tired and discouraged. The beige cotton dress had lost its crisp lines. Her makeup needed freshening and her feet ached.

Tomorrow was another day. All she wanted to do now was head for home and a long afternoon nap, followed by a refreshing swim.

The weather was delightfully sunny and, at least so far, clear of summer rain clouds. She wondered if Seb had walked down to the cottage and knocked, expecting to find her. "We'll talk tomorrow," he had said, and she knew what he meant: *We'll talk about us.*

She guessed that Sebastian Farleigh hadn't had many brush-offs in his life, and she wondered how he'd accept this one. She had wanted to be friends—probably even more than friends—but not with someone dealing in drugs. Never that. Kingpin or mere pusher, it didn't matter, they were all smeared with the same filth.

She had to be honest with herself, though, and admit that the man had attracted her. Quite a lot, too, considering. She'd been almost ready for a new love, but she was cutting this one off right now while she still had freedom of choice.

At an open-air lunch counter on the beach she ordered a sandwich and iced coffee. The couple across from her was holding hands, and when the man put an arm around the girl and began to whisper in her ear, Ariana looked quickly away.

She finished the coffee, then wrapped her ham sandwich carefully in several white paper napkins before tucking it away in her purse. It was just too hot to eat anything now, but with some fruit and raw carrot sticks it would do nicely for her supper. And anyway, making ends meet had better begin at once, if finding work was going to be this hard.

She saw the sign as she turned the car onto the boulevard. "Come to Paradise," it invited. "Follow next side road. Five miles."

Well, and why not? She wanted more time to think before she saw Seb again, anyway.

*

Ariana bought her ticket of admission and walked through tall, arching masses of apricot- and salmon-colored bougainvillea into Paradise. Everywhere that she could see were flowering shade trees, tall pines, rare palms, and tropical flora so exotic she could not even guess at their identities. The perfume of a dozen different blossoms mingled in the salt-scented air.

Paradise was alive with rainbow-colored birds—brilliantly plumaged macaws flying free, splendid crested cockatoos on posing perches, rare parrots and cockatiels in airy cages suspended from fruit-laden branches of avocado and mango trees. Along marked pathways strolled the visitors, content to be, for a little while, part of the fragrant beauty of the tranquil acres.

Beyond this spectacular area, which included an attractive gift shop and a posing spot for photographing the birds, were the gems of Paradise—five smaller gardens, each featuring trees, vines, bushes, and plants of a specific color range. As the seasons changed, so too did the blossoms, but always within the same color scheme. Paradise was world-renowned for these five tropical examples of landscaping art named "White on White," "Lavender's Blue," "Sunshine Place," "Mixed Palette," and "Blossomtime."

Ariana's wide-eyed gaze found a walkway labeled Allamanda Trail, and she followed the path of the lemon-colored bell flowers into a golden enclosure. Sitting quietly on a bench in the yellow garden called Sunshine Place, she rested under the beauty of the delightful *Cassia fistula* blooms that draped a canopy of fragile golden clusters against the blue of the sky, admired the lovely ginger lilies in stately summer glory, and heard the hum of insects among dainty *Ipomea* vines and the blossoms of the Cup of Gold.

It was a blissful place. She rested her head against the smooth gray trunk of the slender *Cassia* and closed her eyes. An old, shabbily dressed man caught her dreaming there.

He moved quietly to the next bench and sank down, exhausted. Ariana roused and saw him. Her eyes anxious, she whispered, "Are you all right?"

His eyelids flickered. "Felt faint . . . better now." His

faded blue eyes inspected her with interest. "Frightened you, did I? I'm sorry, lassie. It's better already," he said, resting his silver head against the back of the bench again.

Ariana was silent for a few moments, observing the trembling of the old man's hands and what seemed to her to be an almost dangerous pallor. "Did you have lunch? I mean, have you eaten today?"

His bushy white eyebrows rose. Light blue eyes studied her face. "Not lunch exactly."

She said worriedly, "Nor breakfast either, I imagine. You're *that* pale. That's not good, you know." Out from the beige purse came the ham-on-whole-wheat. "I brought a sandwich with me that I want you to share, and I don't want any argument about it. I'm out of work myself and looking for a job, so I understand how things can be. It's nothing to be ashamed of, you know. The important thing is that we can help each other."

She divided the sandwich, keeping a small piece for herself so he would not argue and waste more energy. "Please," she said. "You'll feel so much better when you have some food in you."

The old man hesitated. "The sign says no food or drink, doesn't it?"

"Oh, fiddle." She glanced around. "No one's watching, and if they should come, I'll just tell them that it's my fault. That I made you do it." Her warm smile was encouraging. "I'll tidy up the crumbs and napkins so neatly when we're through that no one will ever guess we broke a rule."

He settled back on the bench, munching contentedly, and Ariana sat silently next to him in their small oasis of peace and beauty. "Besides," she said a little later, "anyone who could create a place as lovely as Paradise would understand. It's so beautiful."

The man wiped his mouth neatly on one of the paper napkins, and inclined his head in a gracious little gesture.

"It's the loaf of bread, the jug of wine, and thou beside me . . ."

His hands had nearly stopped their trembling, Ariana noted with satisfaction. She wondered how far he had come in his shabby tennis shoes and cheap cotton trousers, and whether she should offer to drive him home. If he had a home, that is—

"Do you come here often?" she asked him, her brown eyes warm with concern.

The old man had almost finished the sandwich now, and he turned his head to glance at her. "As often as I can. Beauty is food for the soul. You find it so?"

"Oh, yes! This really is a paradise, isn't it? I suppose in the winter season it's quite filled with tourists, but all of it has been landscaped so wisely with these small, secluded garden spots that it would hold the illusion of quietness even then."

He nodded in agreement and looked up into the branches of the graceful Golden Shower tree. " 'A thing of beauty is a joy forever,' " he quoted. " 'Its loveliness increases . . .' Do you know Keats, my dear?"

"A little. Enough to recognize the start of his *Endymion.*" She suggested, "When you finish the sandwich, let's go back to the gift shop annex and buy a cup of coffee, shall we? My treat."

He said simply, "You are one of the good people of this world, aren't you?" He touched her hand and then gave a faint sigh. "Here comes—"

The dark-haired man bearing swiftly down upon them had the definite air of being the person in charge. His expression was heavily disapproving, and Ariana reached guiltily for the paper napkins, thankful that the last of the ham sandwich was even now disappearing into her companion's mouth.

Ignoring her presence completely, the young man strode forward angrily and caught the old man by the arm. "I thought I told you—" he began authoritatively, and Ariana sprang protectively into action.

"Don't you dare touch him! He hasn't done anything. It was my fault, I gave him the sandwich. And we haven't hurt a thing. See? not even a napkin tossed on the ground. I want to see the manager," she insisted. "I can explain everything."

The old man exhaled deeply. "Carlos is the management, lassie," he said. "He has not come to toss me rudely out of Paradise, but rather to admonish me for being here when I had strict orders to be elsewhere. Am I correct, Carlos?"

Carlos's voice still held the accent of his native Cuba. "You promised me most faithfully that you'd rest if I let you weed that patch of tropical iris," he said softly. "And where do I find you?"

Ariana said deliberately, "He's an old man and needs a longer lunch period than younger workers. If you're the manager, you should see to it. He needs time to eat and then time to rest."

Shakily, the old man reached out his hand to her. She patted it comfortingly and glared at the manager who glanced, puzzled, from one face to the other.

"Mr. Ferguson is the owner, not one of the workers here," he said abruptly.

The old man stirred and came slowly to his feet, clutching Ariana's arm. "But Carlos gives the orders," he admitted. "And he's quite right, of course. I did promise to rest. But meeting you has been a joy, my dear. Will you walk back with me to the office?"

"Come along," said Carlos, leading the way out of the yellow garden. Mr. Ferguson and Ariana followed more slowly, past the many planters filled with orchids, past frangipani trees and the great banks of gardenias, up past the cages of tropical birds to the office, which was cleverly constructed as an almost-hidden extension of the cypress-planked gift shop.

With exquisite courtesy Mr. Ferguson seated her in a handsome wing-backed chair upholstered in soft tan leather. Carlos stood frowning until the old man sank down on the matching sofa and swung up his feet. "Order coffee for us, please, Carlos?" The younger man nodded, using an interoffice telephone to give the order to someone in the gift shop.

"I was going to offer to drive you home," Ariana said with a bit of embarrassment in her voice. Her fingers stroked the soft leather of the chair. "But I can see now that won't be necessary. You *are* home, aren't you? And in good hands, too, so I'll just tell you again how beautiful Paradise is, and that I hope you feel much better very soon, and I'll be on my way."

Carlos looked surprised. "You'll stay and share our coffee, please? We'd both like that."

Mr. Ferguson nodded. "The lassie's job-hunting, Carlos. It occurs to me that we'd find no better person for our own opening in the shop."

Ariana saw Carlos's brief hesitation. "Elena's already had her two weeks' holiday. We'd decided to wait until November, remember? We can manage nicely through October. Are you from this area, Miss—?"

"Radnor," she answered. "Ariana Radnor. I moved here recently from Colorado. I'd be glad to leave my phone number with you in case you do decide to hire someone before November, and I can furnish recommendations, naturally. Meanwhile, I'll keep looking."

"A Welsh lassie," Mr. Ferguson said dreamily. "I think we should have her."

Carlos said, "We need someone who's bilingual."

"Would French do? And a little German—only college-level German, I'm afraid, but still useful."

"Very impressive," Carlos said sharply. He passed her a cup of coffee. "Cream? sugar?"

"This is fine, thank you."

"We'd have to see the references first. Have you done any gift shop saleswork before, Miss Radnor?"

She admitted, "Not exactly, but I've worked with the public since I finished college four years ago."

"Hire her, lad, and be done with it. She's honest, anyone can see that, and she's compassionate—she shared her food with me. Our birds and flowers need people with compassion around them."

Carlos smiled wryly. "You're supposed to be asleep. No gardening at all for you tomorrow, hear me? And if Miss Radnor comes to us, it is as assistant to Elena in the gift shop, not as Freddy's helper."

The old man grinned.

Carlos opened a desk drawer and reached in for an application form and a pencil. "With the mail as slow as it is, have you telephone numbers we could use now to get oral recommendations? The written ones can follow." He smiled at her and his dark brown eyes were friendlier. "He'll give me no peace until we finish this, Miss Radnor."

Ariana's face glowed with hope. "Oh yes, of course I can give you phone numbers, and I think I'd like to work in your gift shop, very much in fact."

"You'd be free to start the first of the month?" he asked, getting up to go out and call Montval from another telephone. "If this checks out okay, I mean."

She nodded vigorously, and he lifted a hand in mock salute to the old man, who quickly shut his eyes and pretended not to have seen it at all.

Carlos was back within fifteen minutes, an amused look on his dark face. "You pass," he said. "Would you like their messages now or later?"

"Oh now, please."

Carlos reviewed the paper in his hand. "Emma French sends you her love and us her congratulations if you should decide to work for us."

Ariana heard the soft chuckle from the leather sofa.

"The general manager's executive secretary, Lucy

Welles, endorsed all your credentials and said you also make a great roommate." Carlos's dark eyes considered her thoughtfully. "Interesting information. And there's a third message from a Mrs. Laura Barton, who says she misses your companionship when she rides, and that she'd consider transferring to Paradise if we had a decent cavvy of horseflesh and not a mess of noisy parrots."

Mr. Ferguson sat up. "Barton? Laura Barton of Barton Transportation Corporation?"

Ariana wasn't sure. "She's a widow, and I wouldn't know about the corporation part. I think her husband had taxicabs or a limousine service. Something like that."

The silver head nodded. "And trains and planes and ships and trucking lines. Well, good for old Laura, glad to hear she's still alive." He was reclining on the sofa again, eyes closed. "Long ago, before a certain war, Laura's granddaughter was engaged to my son."

The paneled office grew very still. From outside the air-conditioned room Ariana could faintly hear the cries of the brilliant macaws and the gorgeous cockatoos.

Mr. Ferguson said, "I think I will sleep a while. Carlos, you take Ariana around, introduce her to the staff, things like that." He gave her his thin hand in farewell. "Lassie, I'm glad we found you. You brightened the day."

Some tender bit of feeling rose in Ariana's throat, and she bent down and brushed the wrinkled cheek with her cool lips. "Good-bye, Mr. Ferguson. I've loved meeting you. I'll see you again quite soon." Her eyes were misty as she followed Carlos through the office door and into the warmth of the late afternoon.

They started off for the gift shop, with Carlos explaining working hours, rotating weekends, salary, and the various fringe benefits she could expect, as they walked along. "I'm Carlos de Mesa, and I'm the boss. You will call me Carlos, and you'll answer to Ariana. It's first names all the way around here except for Mr. Ferguson."

"He's not well, is he? He looks so frail."

"Heart. His wife is dead and he lost his only son in the Korean War. He has a married daughter up in Canada and a couple of grandkids, but they don't get down often. He lives for this place. Paradise is all that keeps him going." He held the gift shop door open for her. "They don't make them any finer than Mr. Ferguson. Hey, Elena," he called to the dark, sultry brunette who was checking merchandise in a showcase. "Come and meet your new assistant. Elena Martines—Ariana Radnor."

The girl was a beauty, about twenty-two, Ariana decided, and she had a fantastic figure. She was speaking to Carlos in rapid Spanish, and he touched her arm firmly. "English, Elena, English."

The girl shrugged her shoulders. "When does she begin?" she asked, looking meltingly at Carlos. "I thought we had agreed to wait until the fall before hiring again?"

She's in love with him, Ariana thought. And she doesn't like me. "I think I start the first of September," she answered quietly.

"Have you seen Freddy?" Carlos inquired.

Elena pouted. "That showoff! Just like his birds. He's at lunch. Ken, too. Summer business is slow, Carlos. Why two salesladies?"

"One so pretty and fair, one so pretty and dark. Good for business." He chucked her under her rounded chin. "It will also give you more time to talk to me."

She brightened. "Carlos, you are coming over tonight? Mama has *arroz con pollo* for supper."

Ariana and Carlos were on their way again. He called back to the girl, "Yes, thank you, but I'll be late. Work."

She made a face. "Always night work." She raised a languid hand in answer to Ariana's good-bye. "Come early on the first. You have much to learn."

Carlos steered her to the left, past a little lake and the birds' night quarters, to a cypress ranch-style house built amidst a stand of tall pines. "Oh, lovely," Ariana exclaimed.

"Private quarters, Mr. Ferguson's. The staff has a lounge on the side; the grounds crew—all twenty of them under Armando's direction—have a place by the parrots' night quarters. That's where the feed is stored, too, plus medical supplies for the birds, fertilizers and such. The orchid houses are over there to your right. See them? They're partly obscured by that belt of palms. All this is out-of-bounds to the patrons, of course. Visitors follow the paths and the arrows and the outlined side trips to the various gardens. All plants, shrubs, trees and vines are labeled, with common name, botanical name, and native country. The caged birds likewise."

"I know. I bought a ticket early this afternoon and took the self-guided tour. That's where I met Mr. Ferguson—in the little yellow garden called Sunshine Place, where the benches back up against the Golden Shower trees. He looked so ill that I was worried. I thought he was hungry." She could smile at that now.

"Hungry?"

"Oh, you know—as if he maybe didn't have enough money for a meal."

A wide smile lit up Carlos's face.

Ariana sputtered, "Well, have you looked at his shoes lately? How was I to know, I ask you." She grinned. "I offered him a sandwich."

"And he ate it?" Carlos asked. "No wonder you two looked guilty as sin when I came hunting him." He took her elbow and guided her down two steps and into a colorful, pleasant lounge.

Two men were seated at the table, and Carlos pulled out a chair for Ariana. "Ken, Freddy. We're joining you, what's for lunch?"

Out of a small galley of a kitchen came a tall thin black woman in a spotless white uniform. "You ought to know, you made up the menus with me. Cream of cauliflower soup, tossed salad, and chicken sandwiches." She smiled at

Ariana. "You're new here? Choice of iced tea, coffee, tea, or milk. Flan for dessert."

Carlos said, "Mr. Ferguson's had part of his lunch, Florence. He's resting now, probably will sleep for an hour or so. When I go back, I'll take him a tray with salad and flan. This is Ariana Radnor, she's going to help Elena in the gift shop. Ariana, this is the best cook in the whole of Nassau, Florence Porter. Mr. Ferguson stole her from Government House ten years ago, and he's never dared go back since."

Florence extended her hand in welcome. Next Carlos introduced her to affable Freddy Messina, the parrot trainer, and to Freddy's more serious assistant, Ken Smith. Then, while Carlos went off with Florence to get his lunch and a cup of tea for Ariana, Freddy introduced her to an older man who had just entered the lounge. "Armando Rivas, he's head of grounds and gardens and is a master in orchid culture."

Carlos reminded her that there were a few more staff members who were away on summer vacations, and a big grounds crew, too. "You'll meet them later on. Right now," he suggested, "why don't you finish your tea and go with Freddy to get a behind-the-scenes look at the parrots?"

Ariana hesitated. "Do you have everything you need from me—social security number, all those things?"

"All set," he assured her. "Anything that's lacking we can fill in on the day you report for work."

She waved good-bye to Florence and Armando, and turned to go with Freddy. "Mr. Ferguson's got this thing about poetry," Freddy was explaining. "All the birds get fancy names like Shelley, Byron, and Wordsworth. That Scarlet Macaw—the gaudy red and yellow and blue gentleman over there—is Keats. He's from Bolivia. He's also the star performer of the Paradise Parade. That's what we call the little show Ken and I put on for the tourists three times a day, with macaws, parrots, and cockatoos as the performing artists."

They were standing by the large flight aviary for the macaws. Ken Smith was inside, in the process of removing them, two by two, to the posing stands near the gift shop. Ken would lower a long wooden rod, call two of the macaws by name, and the tamed birds would obediently mount the perch to be carried off. Each time Ken spoke quietly to the birds, taking a moment with each one, using its name and assuring it gently that all was well.

"He's good with the macaws," Freddy said. "Real gentle, yet definitely in charge."

When Keats's turn came to be transferred, the Scarlet Macaw stepped rather gracefully onto the perch and stood there, flapping his wings energetically. Ariana gasped. "Oh, he's beautiful, and so big!"

Freddy agreed proudly. "The macaws are the largest members of the parrot family. Keats there measures almost three feet, of which half that length is his impressive tail. His wingspread is thirty-six inches. But come and meet Pete now. He's not half so spectacular to see, but I'll wager he's one of the most intelligent parrots I've ever worked with."

Ariana watched Ken walk off with Keats calmly sharing the transfer rod with a Blue and Gold Macaw named Milton, whose daily morning duty, Freddy solemnly assured her, was to salute the American flag at reveille. "Oh, really?" she asked, wondering if her jocular companion wasn't just teasing a greenhorn.

"It's the truth," he said. "Our show's pretty good, but it's nothing compared with the one at the Parrot Jungle down in Miami, of course. They're the real pros in the business, and you ought to visit there someday. But ours isn't bad at all, considering that the main attraction at Paradise is, and always has been, its five tropical gardens. I imagine the Parrot Jungle in Miami has some thousand birds or more; we have not quite a hundred. It should be 102 by tomorrow, though. If we're lucky."

"You're buying more?"

"Hatching out a few Leadbetter's Cockatoos. We hope. They're called Pink Cockatoos in their native Australia, really gorgeous birds. Next time you're here I'll show you the nesting boxes."

A clear call rang through the air. "Hello, Freddy! Hello, Freddy!"

Ariana's astonishment was complete. She stood there, mouth open, shaking her head in disbelief, as Freddy returned the eager greeting of the pale gray parrot in the cage suspended from a low branch of a pink-blossomed *Bauhinia monandra* tree.

"Hello, Pete. Having a good day?"

"Hello, Freddy. Fair."

"Come on, Ariana, close your mouth," drawled Freddy, laughing softly at her. "It's only a bird. An African Grey Parrot. Come a little closer, move in slowly, and don't lift your hands yet."

"Oh dear," she whispered, following his instructions. "What's the matter with his leg?"

"It's splinted with a large feather quill. That's why he's isolated down here in a hospital cage with only one low perch. Pete's leg was broken about two days ago. We hoped it would heal naturally, but I soon saw that we'd have to splint it to avoid a possible amputation. Pete's a valuable bird, one of our best talkers, and we're hoping this will do the trick."

"How long before you'll know?"

Freddy had opened the cage and was gently stroking the parrot's back with two fingers. "Good old Pete, good boy. This way, it should heal within ten days," he answered, reaching into his pocket for a slice of fresh apple. "Watch this, Ariana.

"Radnor. Radnor. Radnor." Freddy repeated Ariana's last name several times, speaking clearly and slowly. "One or two syllable names are best, so we'll use your last name, and not Ariana."

The African Grey tilted his head to one side. The pale straw-colored eyes held a whimsical expression.

"Radnor," said Freddy.

"Radnor," repeated Pete.

Freddy passed the apple fragment to Ariana. "Lift your hand slowly and offer him the fruit. He won't bite you. I'll keep my hand right here, too, to help him hold the apple. With that splinted leg he's a bit handicapped."

Pete graciously accepted her offering. "Radnor," said Freddy again.

"Radnor," agreed the parrot.

The trainer closed the cage, securing the lock carefully. "Bye, Pete."

The bird had a wistful look now, Ariana thought. "Bye, Freddy. Call the cops," he added mournfully.

"I wish I could stay, he looks so lonesome," Ariana said. "But it's after five and I must head on home." They were walking up the Allamanda Trail, passing cages and aviaries of exotic birds on their way back to the entrance.

The worried look on Freddy's naturally happy face was very apparent. "I wish you could stay, too. Pete took to you, I could tell that right away. He's a highly intelligent little fellow, and this broken leg's doubly hard on him for he likes to be where the action is. But when I put him up by the others, he tries to join in the show, and then his leg suffers. Yet if I keep him away from the other birds, he hears them and feels very left out of things, pulls at his splint tapes, and all that. I'm afraid he might have a nervous breakdown."

Ariana gave him a shrewd look. "You're kidding."

"No," he said, "actually I'm not. Trained birds can go into a kind of decline. They're really sensitive creatures. Pete was going great in his vocabulary training, and now he won't even practice his theme song because it was a part of his act in the show."

Theme song? Ariana was skeptical. "You don't mean he sings, do you? Talk, yes, I believe it because I heard it myself. But *sing?*"

"He sings." Freddy crooned the opening bars of "Moon over Miami." "Like that."

Ariana laughed so hard that tears stood in her eyes. "Oh no, wait until Lucy hears this, that I'm going to be working for a singing parrot! Freddy, you've made my day. Thanks for the tour, friend. See you bright and early September first."

*

The gate swung open easily, and she drove through, hopped out to lock it again, and headed up the drive to her own small parking area. Not yet six, she thought with satisfaction, smelling the sea and glad to be back.

The westering sun touched the coral rock of her cottage with a golden brilliance. Overhead, gulls called and wheeled in great circles against the summer-blue sky. She sat there, looking at the little house, and knew a wonderful feeling of having come home. She felt comforted and secure, as she had not done since saying good-bye to the familiar house where she had lived with her parents. Everything was going to turn out all right, she told herself. Bless Aunt Margaret and her gift of the bolthole.

Seb came striding purposefully down the path and yanked open the car door. "And where the devil have you been all day?" he demanded to know.

She scrambled out. "In Delray, looking for a job. I *told* you, Seb."

"Not that you'd be gone today, you didn't." Blue eyes, dark with relief, searched her face. "My God, if I have to watch out for you, too—"

She turned quickly away, reaching into the car for her purse. He caught her arm and pulled her back to face him. "Answer me, damn it, did you?"

"Let go of my arm, Seb," she said coldly, starting up the path. "Did I what?"

"Did you have any luck in Delray?"

She replied calmly, "No luck at all in Delray Beach."

"Too bad." He looked at her sharply. "You might at least have left me a note, stuck it by the doorknob there, if you couldn't take the time to telephone before you left."

She nodded, unlocking the dutch door. "Yes, I could have, couldn't I? If I'd wanted to— But don't you remember my telling you that I didn't plan to be a burden? You needn't have worried about me."

She turned toward him to say goodnight, but Seb moved quickly, lifting her over the threshold into the cottage and closing the door after them. "I shouldn't have thought it would be a question of burden, after last night?"

"Mm, last night," she said regretfully. "Last night there was a moon, and I felt lonely. Perhaps you did, too."

Blue eyes flashed a warning. "Just that?" His hands reached out and caught her to him. She struggled, and he drew her closer still, so close that she could hear his heartbeats where her cheek was buried against his chest. He dropped his chin to the top of her shining head. "So last night meant nothing to you, Ariana?" he asked grimly, turning her in his arms, lifting her face to meet his lips. His mouth was warm against her own, his kisses light and coaxing. Then, as he felt her tremble, he drew her close again, crushing her against the long length of him. His mouth came down hungrily on her own—seeking, demanding, finding response.

When he straightened up, his hands still gripped her shoulders. Dazed with emotion, she told him, "You can let go. I'm not going to fall." Her fair hair swung forward, concealing her face, and he gently brushed the silky strands back and lifted her chin.

"I've been half-crazy with worry today," he muttered,

tracing the lovely curve of her cheek with a cool, lean finger. "Don't ever do anything like that to me again."

She pushed his hand away. "Seb, don't rush me . . . I'm not ready to get involved. I don't want to fall in love again or—or anything." She heard the sudden inrush of his breath. "I don't think I even know what love really is."

He stared at her. "I'm sorry," she murmured haltingly. "But I mean what I said, Seb."

"It's all right," he said gently. "There's plenty of time for us ahead. I'll not rush you, Ariana, and that's a promise." The way he was looking at her tied knots through the nerves in her stomach. "Someday," he said, and smiled.

"I can't promise. Don't ask me to promise anything."

He brushed the lightest of kisses on her forehead. "What's for dinner?" he asked. "Somehow I never got around to lunch today. Look, why don't you get out of those townie clothes. While you shower, I'll start us an omelette. I've got salad and fresh strawberries up at the Court."

He gave her a grin that turned her heart upside down again. Now was the time, she thought, to ask him about the little plastic bags. Now, while they were looking at each other this way and liking what they saw—and before they had traveled so far along the way that a parting would hurt . . . rather dreadfully.

"Seb," she began, stepping out of her emerald sandals and moving off toward the bathroom. "Seb, can you hear me from in here?"

"Yes." He had found milk in the refrigerator, located a beater and bowls, and was counting out the eggs. "Five— six, perhaps? Did you have lunch?"

She left the bathroom door ajar a little as she undressed. "No. Yes. That is, I bought a sandwich at noon, but I just wasn't hungry right then, and much later I shared it with an old man."

He separated the first egg into the two bowls and shouted toward the door. "You're joking."

"No," she laughed. "A nice old man. My new boss. I thought he was hungry, you see." She poked her head around the door and saw his hands go very still.

Blue eyes met hers accusingly. "Your new boss? You said you hadn't found a job."

She pulled on her robe and came barefoot out to him. "No," she protested, "that isn't what I said. You came on so strong out there that I was a bit miffed, and when you asked me if I'd had any luck in Delray, I told you no, not in Delray."

His dark brows had drawn together and he was glaring at her again, eyes ablaze. Tension mounted in her and she whispered uncertainly, "Seb, what's wrong? Why do you look at me like that?"

He asked sharply, "Then you did find work?"

"I was telling you," she stammered, feeling a sensation of complete helplessness. "The old man with whom I shared my sandwich—James Ferguson, his name is—he hired me to work in the gift shop at Paradise."

"At *Paradise?*"

"It's a tourist attraction. A nice one, Seb. All orchids and lovely gardens and some tropical birds, parrots mostly."

He interrupted bluntly, "I know the place. I won't have you working there, Ariana. Tomorrow you will telephone and—"

"Wait a minute," she said, stung by his attitude. *"You* won't have me working there?"

He ignored her outraged expression. "You heard me. If you had any sense you'd realize why. You've barely escaped a nervous breakdown, Ariana. You need to find a position with regular hours, a quiet routine, something not in the public eye."

"Ah, yes," she said, sarcasm heavy in her voice. "A job like the one in Coral Gables, no doubt. Receptionist and some typing, wasn't it? Well, let me tell you, Sebastian Farleigh, I *liked* Paradise. I *liked* Carlos and Mr. Ferguson and I *liked* the parrots, and I'm starting work there a week from last Monday, on September first at nine o'clock."

His voice sounded bleak. "Suppose that I asked you not to, just to please me? Would you agree?"

"I don't think so," she said wearily, regret heavy in her tones. "You see, it's so important to me, Seb—important to find a job by myself, to prove to myself that I can make it on my own."

His face looked hard with the lips gone thin like that. She caught her breath. "Suppose I won't allow you to work there?" he said. "What then?"

That shocked her, and he knew it. He tried to put his arms around her, but she backed off. She would not be intimidated by this man, especially by this man. "You couldn't stop me, Seb. Not unless there was a very good reason."

He raised his dark eyebrows. "And what if I said that there was a good reason, but that you'd have to take it on trust, for I couldn't tell you . . . take me on trust, too." He seized her wrists.

Regretfully, she shook her head. "I can't, Seb. I almost wish I could, but I can't."

His blue eyes shadowed with a kind of pain. She was struggling futilely to free herself from his grasp when he let her go, suddenly, so that she stumbled back, almost losing her balance. "That's that, then," he said.

Savagely, he flung the door open and was gone. With tears on her cheeks, Ariana returned the milk and eggs to the refrigerator and went back to the bathroom to have her shower.

*

It was dark by the time the dishes from her evening meal were washed and put away in the cupboard. She glanced at the kitchen clock and was surprised to see that it was well after nine. Restless, she wandered out onto the deck, closed her eyes and listened to the lonely sound of an evening sea. The moonlight tugged at her heart, and the fragrance of the night flowers seemed almost too haunting to bear.

She left the deck and sought the moonlit path over the dunes to the beach, where she leaned her cheek against the rough trunk of a coconut palm and just stood there, with the night breeze catching her hair so that it blew back in silken streamers. Desperately lonely, she walked the stretch of beach, feeling tears dry in salty streaks on her face. Returning more slowly, she found a grassy ridge on the dune near the cottage and lay down there, with her elbows dug into the sandy earth and her chin resting in her cupped palms, staring bleakly out to sea. Thinking—

Thinking how passing strange it was that Ron was now just the ghost of a love—that in less than five weeks his power to hurt her, to make her weep, bereft, was gone. Even the grief over lost love was gone now, leaving only a little sadness that would heal in time, and heal like a clean wound with no festering.

Had it ever been real love at all? she wondered.

Once, years ago, she had come home from a high school dance and anxiously asked her mother how a girl could know for sure when she was in love. And her mother, smiling, had replied that if you had to wonder about it, wonder even a little bit, it wasn't love.

Yet if Seb walked down the beach now and stretched out his arms to her, she knew what she would do—she'd go to him, running, her heart in her hands . . . And that was the problem, for this wonderful new feeling for Seb hadn't a prayer of a chance for happiness, either, she thought sadly, not if what she suspected about Seb turned out to be true.

CHAPTER 7

Fatigue and reaction caught up with Ariana the next day and she treated herself to a lazy morning, lying in bed until her stomach begged for breakfast, and then casually leafing through magazines until the clock reached eleven and she could telephone Emma in her office, two time zones away.

Emma was delighted that she was taking the job at Paradise. "You're getting back on your feet," Emma rejoiced. "All you needed was a rest, honey." She told Ariana that Carlos had a voice smoother than fine brandy. "Watch that man," she warned jokingly. "He'd make a heady lover." She gave Ariana all the latest Montval news, casually sliding in the information that Ron had married and taken his new bride off to Europe.

"Or vice versa," Ariana quipped, and she heard Emma's relieved sigh.

Afterward, Ariana got in her car and drove to Hibiscus. She checked her post office box and found the money order that Lucy had sent after selling Ariana's blue VW. That was good news. She bought fresh vegetables, some fruit and milk, and then drove home and spent hours cleaning the cottage, which didn't need it, but it was either that or doing something strenuous like kneading bread dough, and it was much too warm today to have the oven on.

It was really too warm to do much of anything, but she kept at the chores doggedly, even while the locksmith was there. All afternoon she worked with a determined intensity, refusing to let her mind wander from the cottage and the various tasks at hand.

Only later did she allow herself to think of Seb. She sat on the beach, hugging her drawn-up knees, and watched the waves come creaming up between her bare toes.

She wasn't in love with Seb, she reminded herself firmly. Not yet. Of course she wasn't. You couldn't fall in love that fast, could you? She was no off-again-on-again sort of girl. What she felt for Seb was undoubtedly just the normal physical attraction of a girl for a good-looking man.

And that was all it had better ever be, she promised herself, wading out into the gentle surf and swimming lazily just off the shallows. It was deliciously cool in the ocean. Next time she was in Delray she was going to buy a mask and snorkel. Flippers, too.

Absorbed in her thoughts, she rolled over and floated, watching the sun start down towards sunset. The jetty was empty. Disappointment welled up inside her. Her eyes followed the channel markers out to sea. No sign of a boat—

By the time she returned to the cottage she was fighting an urge to march right up to the Court for some straight talk with one Sebastian Farleigh. And that would not do at all, so in a panic she showered and dressed, touched her favorite Worth perfume to her wrists and earlobes, and practically ran down to her car, driving hastily off to Delray Beach. With the promise of a job, and money from the VW's sale already on the way to the bank, she determined to treat herself to dinner out and perhaps a movie.

Three hours later she unlocked her cottage. She shrugged her shoulders helplessly. There was no denying it—Seb had been on her mind all evening, his dear face coming between her and the screen throughout the entire film.

Swiftly, she changed her shoes, sliding out of the smart

beige pumps and into flat, white leather thongs. If she didn't go to Seb and ask questions, settle once and for all time these suspicions in her mind, she would never get to sleep at all that night. She knew that.

She admitted, too, that she wasn't being fair to him either—condemning him like this without giving him the slightest chance to defend himself, to explain away the little plastic envelopes. One way or another, she had to see Seb. She had to see him and talk to him.

Her pretty face full of concern, she let herself out by way of the french doors, hearing the reassuring click of the new lock. Behind her in La Casita's living room two lamps glowed. She felt quite safe, walking up the graveled drive to the Court, with the thick green foliage of the spiky carissa shrubbery high above her head on both sides and a lopsided piece of moon in the sky. Crossing the lawns she needed her flashlight, and she flicked the torch off and on at intervals. At no time did she make a special effort to be quiet.

Once she thought she saw a rabbit. The tiny night creature fled off, startled.

Her steps slowed a bit as the Court came in view, its peaked tiled roofs silhouetted dark against the sky. She wished now that she had telephoned ahead. "I'm on my way up," she should have told him. "Come and meet me?"

And he would have, too. She was sure of that.

Ahead of her was the low stone wall, with the terrace just beyond. She sat down on the top of the wall and swung her legs over with a graceful movement, hearing the rasp of her skirt as rough edges of the stones caught silky threads of fabric. She could see the lights ahead now. Her nostrils caught the subtle fragrance of the satiny pink blossoms of the frangipani trees along the terrace, the long-blooming *Plumeria* whose upright branches gave the effect of a huge candelabrum reaching toward the sky.

Clouds covered the moon. She turned the flashlight on

the ground near her feet, walking carefully across the last few yards to the wide steps of the terrace. The night had turned hazy, with swirling wisps of fog drifting in from the ocean, but through the sliding glass doors she could see straight into Seb's living room, and she paused, flicking off the torch and retreating a step or two until the metal frame of a terrace lounge chair touched the backs of her legs.

Two men were seated by a low coffee table in the room, examining something spread out before them. Seb stood to one side, watching intently. In a nearby chair facing the windows lounged a beautiful young woman, lamplight shining on brown hair so dark it gleamed black. She was looking up at Seb, who had bent down to the table. Ariana saw the glint of metal in his hands. A small gun—

She gasped.

The girl turned her dark head, staring out into the night. Ariana saw her speak to Seb, and he moved swiftly to the glass doors, sliding one ajar, standing silently in the opening . . . listening. In the shadows Ariana sank silently to her knees, pressing her body tightly against the bulky lounger.

"Nothing." Seb turned back into the room. "Probably a night bird. We can put on the floods, check around—" He reached for his pipe, touched a match to the tobacco in the bowl.

One of the men shook his head. He was heavyset, swarthy. His voice reminded Ariana of Carlos's. "No. No floodlights. Nothing unusual, 'Tian. We've nearly finished here." His hands lingered on the plastic bags before him.

The fair-haired man stretched, easing tense muscles. "We'll take these then. Ready, Tony?"

The young woman came gracefully to her feet. She pointed to the table. "Are you leaving Seb some samples?"

"For God's sake, no! My housekeeper's due back tomorrow. Get everything out of here."

"You running nervy, 'Tian?" The dark man laughed. He slid the small envelopes into one of the larger plastic bags, secured the fastening, and lumbered out of his chair.

Ariana slipped from the terrace during their good-byes. Her heart hammered against her ribs as she fled across the gardens and over the low wall. Once out of sight of the Court, she switched on the flashlight and raced down the drive, keeping close to the protective shadows of the hedge.

In the safety of her own house, she leaned back against the door, breathing raggedly, her hands gripping a chair. Still no sound of an automobile coming slowly down the drive toward the entrance gate . . .

She remembered now, there had been no cars parked in the turnaround by the Court. Strange— It was always possible, of course, that Seb's friends had parked some distance off and walked up the drive, or—and Ariana somehow knew this was true—or they had come by boat.

The ringing of the telephone startled her. Thinking fast, she dashed for the bathroom, tore off her clothes, turned on the shower, and grabbed for a towel, catching the telephone on its fifth ring.

"You're puffing," Seb accused her.

"You caught me in the shower. I ran for the phone," she said. "What is it, Seb? I'm dripping all over the carpeting."

"This I want to see. All right if I come down?"

"Don't you dare! Not after the way you stormed out of here yesterday."

"I get these moods," he said coolly. "Been out tonight?"

As if you hadn't checked to be sure. "Mmm. Dinner in town and a movie. Why? Have you been ringing me?"

He asked, "What show did you see?"

Ariana felt a shiver run down her back. "An old Tracy and Hepburn movie. Look, Seb, I'm not dressed for conversation right now, let me call you back."

He persisted. "Which one? When did you get back?"

"It was called *Bringing Up Baby*. And about ten minutes ago," she said stiffly. "Why the third degree? I'm hanging up, Seb."

"I'm coming down."

Frigidly, she told him, "I'm answering no doors tonight, Sebastian Farleigh. I'm tired and I'm going to bed as soon as I finish my shower. Goodnight."

She heard his laughter as she replaced the receiver. And later, as she lay sleepless in bed, she smelled the aroma of pipe tobacco from the deck. She tiptoed to the window and peered out. He was at the far corner, leaning against the cypress railing and looking out to sea.

"Go away!" she hissed.

He answered her without turning his head.

"I can't hear you," she said crossly. "And I'm not listening anyway."

"I said I was sorry about last night." He turned in the direction of her voice. "Meg and Luke arrive tomorrow, Ariana. Rather early, I should imagine. Will you walk up and say hello?"

She considered that for a brief moment. "Of course. About eleven?"

"Fine." There was a pause. "That's what I wanted to talk to you about. They're pretty wonderful folks, and I don't want them fretting because you and I don't seem to get along. So watch it, will you? It would only worry them."

Worry them! If Meg and Luke knew what was really going on, they'd be losing their minds! "I'll remember my manners. Goodnight."

His voice held no amusement. "Goodnight, small one." He started down the deck stairs. "Ariana?"

She snapped, "Now what? Seb, please *go*."

"I'm going. *Je Reviens.* Think about that."

Ariana blinked. *"Bonne nuit,"* she murmured mechanically with throat gone dry. *Good night.*

She pressed her hands together, hardly daring to breathe. She knew what scent she had used earlier that night, touching her wrists and her earlobes with the French perfume as she dressed to go to Delray for dinner. In her mind's eye she could see the round blue bottle on her dresser. Worth's *Je Reviens* . . . I return.

Damn the man! Was he simply telling her that he'd be back, or was he warning her that her *Je Reviens* fragrance had betrayed her to him on the terrace at the Court?

It was just one more worry. And, she thought ruefully, far from explaining matters, tonight's episode at the Court had only further demonstrated Seb's involvement in some unsavory activity. She lay awake for hours—worrying. Toward morning she fell asleep, tossing and turning fitfully, and awoke after ten, heavy-lidded, drained of all energy.

*

Luke was working in the gardens when Ariana walked up the drive. A tall, quiet man in his mid-sixties, he came to greet her with a warm welcoming smile. "Amazing," he admitted. "I think I'd have known you anywhere." He patted the top of her fair head affectionately. "Things are going to seem almost back to normal with young folks around again."

"Luke," she asked him during a break in their conversation, "sometime in the next couple of days would you go into town with me and help me buy a decent used car?"

"You're staying on, then?"

She bit her lip in annoyance. "I don't know why that should surprise everybody."

"It's good news," Luke responded quietly. "Maybe we're too used to bad news lately—" He grinned at her then. "Sure I'll help you with a car, Ariana. Just whistle when you're ready."

He cast an anxious glance back at the gardens. "One month away and they're almost out of control. Summertime the grounds need a firm hand." He shook his head. "Nothing's been done here except the lawn." His impatient look expressed what he thought of the lawn-mowing job. "It's going to take me weeks to get the place in order."

He started slowly back to his work. "Tried to tell Sebastian we shouldn't take a summer vacation. January now, that's a good month to leave the gardens. Never August."

"See you later then, Luke," Ariana called after him. "I'm on my way up to visit a bit with Meg."

He turned around to wave. "She's been waiting to see you. Honey, we're mighty glad you're here."

The housekeeper said almost the same thing, folding Ariana into a warm embrace. "It's a little bit like having Margaret back," she declared, wiping her eyes. "You're so like her."

Meg had brought three women in from Hibiscus to help her. They were washing windows, cleaning screens, waxing floors, and polishing furniture. Up beyond the staircase, Ariana heard the hum of a vacuum cleaner.

"Once I get the place back to normal," Meg said, "I make do with just the occasional help for the heavier jobs. Never could stand people underfoot while I worked." She put her hand on Ariana's shoulder, steering her toward the kitchen wing. "Time for a cup of coffee together," Meg said.

It was like being a little girl again, Ariana thought. She sat on a high kitchen stool, her sandaled feet up on a rung, and watched Meg move efficiently around her domain.

"So you like La Casita?" the gray-haired woman asked, plugging in a percolator, reaching up for cups and saucers.

"Like it? That's mild for how I feel about the cottage. It's perfect. And I know how much you helped, Meg. I found the letter that Aunt Margaret left for me in the sugar bowl." Her voice trailed off a little.

Meg looked up. "She didn't suffer long, honey. She was on her feet up until that last week of her life."

Ariana smiled tremulously. "She left me things that

meant a great deal to her. I think of her each time I see the shell mirror, each time I use her Ming Rose dishes."

"And why not?" the older woman asked brusquely. "You were someone special to Margaret. Maybe she felt about you as if you were the daughter she never had." She poured out the coffee, and offered cream and the coarse beige-colored sugar so many English people prefer. She looked out the window for a moment. "No use calling Luke in. He's *that* upset about the grounds, he'll not take time out for coffee."

They carried their cups to the kitchen table. Meg brought out a plate of cookies. "Store-bought," she sniffed. "High time I was back."

Ariana was sure of that, too. "Where's Seb?" she asked casually.

Meg stirred her coffee. The little silver spoon went around and around and around. When she looked up, her kind blue eyes were shadowed. "Still asleep. He wasn't in yet when we arrived back about five this morning." The silver spoon made a tiny chinking sound as she replaced it in her saucer. "We'd hoped to find him all recovered by the time we got back from our vacation. Seems as though he's looking better, but not all that much."

Ariana said slowly, "He's been ill? Seb?"

Meg looked grim. "You didn't know? No, how could you, unless he told you, and Sebastian's not much for talking about himself." She hesitated. " 'Tweren't just the trial, you know. As if that hadn't been enough—"

Ariana held her breath and the other woman continued slowly. "I don't think he'd really recovered from the blood poisoning when that sinful verdict was handed down. It well nigh killed him. Then Miss Julia's up and breaking their engagement like that—a body can only stand so much."

The sound of a lawn mower approaching the kitchen windows filled the room. Meg went out to check on the cleaning, and Ariana rested her head against the wall and closed her eyes. *Trial?*

When Meg came back, she asked, "What trial? Start at the beginning."

Meg's voice dropped. "You're practically one of the family. I guess it isn't gossiping to tell you if you don't know."

Ariana said firmly, "It's not gossiping. I haven't the faintest idea what it's all about, and yes, I should know, Meg."

"Margaret didn't mention it then," Meg acknowledged. "The whole business disgusted her so, and it started just about the time Mr. Cecil first got so sick, about four years ago, I'd say. They were in England then. By the time Mr. Cecil had died and Margaret was back here, fixing up your little place and so happy to be doing it, it looked as if there'd be no trial at all. The malpractice screening panel had found no negligence, you see. It ought to have been dropped right then and there, but some big-name lawyer got hold of the Howards and the next thing we knew there was this jury trial."

Ariana was trying to sort out the story. "Wait a minute, Meg. Are you saying Seb was sued in a medical malpractice suit? It's been so long—Margaret somehow never told us Seb had become a physician. I know that's what he hoped to be, years back, but—"

Meg's mouth widened in astonishment. "My soul and body, child, you mean this is *all* news to you? I shouldn't have brought it up had I known that," she admonished herself. "It's just that we love that young man, and we worry so—"

Ariana reached over and touched her hand. "I'm glad you did. I've wondered—he seemed changed."

"Changed? It completely shattered him. He thought they were his friends, you see—the Howards. Jim Howard was Mr. Cecil's chauffeur. Or used to be. Mr. Cecil let him go when he couldn't seem to stop drinking, but Sebastian stayed in touch, helped him a little now and then. Their young Robbie needed surgery—something like a hernia, I think their doctor said. Not too serious a thing at all. They asked Sebastian, and he agreed that it should be fixed because it would give the youngster a better chance. Sebastian arranged it for them, all without charge, you know, every bit of it. He was to give the anaesthetic himself, that's his specialty, of course. He even prepaid the entire hospital bill for them."

"But what happened, Meg?"

Meg's eyes dimmed. "The boy died. I never did understand the medical terms for the problem, something like being allergic to the anaesthetic. To *any* general anaesthetic. A nerve allergy, or something like that, I think it was. He just stopped breathing, and could not be revived. It was nothing anyone could have known in advance. No tests known would have shown that would happen. It was that one surgical chance in a hundred thousand, and it happened to Robbie."

Appalled, Ariana exclaimed, "But surely no one blamed Seb?"

"Not at first. Sebastian was part of the full medical investigation. He felt very bad about the boy's death, Ariana, but he was an excellent anaesthesiologist and had confidence in himself and his judgment. Every physician faces something like that, I suppose, sooner or later in his professional career."

She poured coffee refills for them both. "A short time afterward, he began to get letters. From the Howards." Meg looked uncomfortable. "No one ever told us, Luke and me, but we think the letters threatened Sebastian unless he agreed to make certain payments of money."

"Blackmail?" Ariana felt coldness spread through her. "But that's illegal. Immoral, too."

Meg looked shaken. "I know."

"Then what?"

"Sebastian insisted then on having the whole case go

before a panel—a malpractice screening panel, it's called. There were seven people on the panel, I recall, and they found absolutely no negligence had taken place, and they recommended, as they put it, that the Howards abandon their claim."

Ariana was sitting on the edge of her chair, gripping the cup. "And they didn't?"

"No, they didn't. Maybe it was a deep-seated resentment against Mr. Cecil for firing Jim for alcoholism, and hurting Sebastian was the way they could get even. Luke and I think it was that. Well, whatever it was, Ariana, that lawyer talked to them and they brought suit against Sebastian for millions.

"You've never seen such a display as they put on," Meg said with distaste. "Tears and sobbing and fainting. All the witnesses for Sebastian told the story clear enough, and the screening panel's decision was brought in, too, but with the carrying-on that took place, well, the jury wept with the mother and you can guess how it all ended."

"Oh, poor Seb. Poor Mrs. Howard, too. Nothing would ever compensate for losing a child."

Meg said dryly, "Hard to tell with the Howards. They drove up to the house—the New York one—in a new Cadillac, with Mary Howard all decked out in an expensive mink coat. Said they came by to say good-bye to Luke and me before leaving for California." Tongue in cheek, she added: "We saw to it that they left a mite faster than they'd arrived."

Sadly, Ariana shook her head, thinking of the enormously complex thing that a malpractice suit must be, of the damage to a fine physician's reputation, of Seb's undoubted loss of faith in mankind after something like that. Would it have been so overwhelming as to turn him to drug dealing? she wondered. Somehow that seemed a specially evil thing for a doctor to do.

"You said he'd been ill, too?"

Meg nodded. "The court case seemed to drag on and

on. Almost two years, I recall. Sebastian found it difficult
to relax, ever. Luke and he went fishing over in the Baha-
mas one week, and Sebastian tore his arm on some coral.
That's always potentially dangerous, you know, and I suppose his general resistance was low about then. He devel-
oped severe blood poisoning and wasn't really back to
good health yet when the court case ended. He came
down here, never returned to his practice. It was as if all
the life went out of that man. Last November, it was.
Maybe now that you've arrived, things will be better,"
Meg concluded hopefully.

She heard movement in the corridor and her mouth
clamped shut in a firm line. Ariana stirred uneasily.

Seb wandered in, looking a little tight-lipped. "Talking
about me?" he asked, his voice brittle.

Meg snapped right back at him. "And if we were, it
would be only good things you'd be hearing. Ready for
your breakfast?"

Ariana stood up. "You're all so busy, I'll leave you to get
on with it. Thanks for your warm welcome, Meg. Sometime I'd like to talk to you some more about Aunt Margaret."

She started past the housekeeper, but Seb put out an
arm and stopped her progress. "Don't go," he said. "Sit
with me while I eat, why don't you? Meg, she doesn't take
time for a decent meal unless someone's looking right
over her shoulder. How about it, Ariana? Join me for
mushrooms on toast and some of that good bacon?"

His eyes dared her to refuse.

*

It was a night as still and haunting as star-scattered dark
velvet. There was just a fraction of moon in the sky. Ariana opened the shutters and sat cross-legged on her bed,
admiring the night. It was good to know that Meg and
Luke were back at the Court. Nice, too, to think that she'd
be at work in two more days.

A soft whistle pierced the night air, followed by the rattle of small pebbles flung onto the flooring of the deck. She padded quickly to the living room and peered out.

"Ariana!" Seb called from the beach. "Come on out!"

She unlatched the french doors and stepped out on the deck. "It's too late. I'm in bed."

"You're not in bed. Put on your suit and come for a swim."

"I told you, it's too late, Seb."

He moved out of the shelter of the palms, a tall shadow of a man, lean hips lapped by a terry towel. "I want to talk to you. It's important. Come down or I'll come up."

She hesitated and was lost. She slipped the white cotton robe over her shorty pajamas, thrust feet into beach sandals, caught up her keys, and climbed the dune to meet him. Hand in hand, they ran down the incline to the sandy beach.

"Come swimming with me. The water's perfect."

The humidity of the day had turned to cool, dark beauty. Chagrined, Ariana looked longingly at the ocean. "I didn't change. I'm still in my pajamas. What was it you wanted to tell me?"

"This," he said, and took her in his arms. She heard the catch of his breath as he tilted her lips toward his mouth. His body was hard against hers, their kiss a sweet searching pleasure.

She felt the warmth of his mouth on her closed eyes, her throat, the little hollow at the base of her neck . . . the touch of his hands at the tie of her robe—

"Well?" he asked, smiling down at her.

"Well?" she whispered, her head nestled on his firm, broad shoulder.

"Swim with me." A flush of wild rose staining her cheeks, she watched his cool, tanned fingers slip the thin garments from her body.

She stood still, arms raised to her breasts, and her heart pounding in furious beats. "You're a lovely woman," he murmured softly. For the briefest of moments his lips touched her bare shoulder, and then he dropped the terry towel from about his waist and reached for her hand.

There was an unashamed naturalness to the night that left her breathless. He was a sea god on the edge of the sea, and they entered the ocean together.

For only a moment she remembered crouching on the shadowed terrace of the Court . . . his cryptic warning . . . and then they were swimming, with her hair trailing loose and silvery in the water, and the moon pale above them as they floated and dived, their bodies touching in passing.

There was a freedom in the velvet darkness such as she had never known before—a oneness with the night and the water. Sculling slowly, she turned on her back and tipped up her head, feeling intensely alive in every cell of her body. "I wish this night would never end," she said, and knew the salty freshness of a kiss as his mouth brushed hers.

"Nothing lasts forever," he told her quietly.

They came out of the sea with water streaming from their bare bodies and the glint of starshine above them. Gently, he wrapped the robe about her.

"Seb?"

His hands crushed water from her dripping hair. Bending, he kissed her sea-cool mouth.

"Seb—" she began again and he drew her close against him.

"Not tonight. No questions tonight," he said. "Let this be a time apart, no more than that, no less." His hands caressed her neck. "Go now."

She looked back when she reached the deck of the cottage, and he was standing motionless as an ancient Grecian statue in the pale moonlight, watching her. Overwhelmed with shyness now, she raised an arm in silent goodnight, and saw him bend to retrieve the towel and start back along the beach toward the Court.

CHAPTER 8

It was raining when Ariana left the cottage to begin her first day of work—a heavy, persistent rain that darkened the sky and drummed on the top of the old yellow VW that Luke had helped her find. The weather bureau predicted clearing skies, however, and assured South Floridians that while a suspicious area of circular wind movement, originally sighted off West Africa, was being carefully monitored, it was far too soon to label it a possible hurricane.

Carlos was waiting near the entrance to Paradise with a huge scarlet umbrella, and he showed her where to park, then escorted her to the gift shop, shielding her from the downpour and explaining cheerfully how badly the gardens needed the rain.

"But it will clear by noon," he predicted with a smile.

Ariana saw Elena's scowl when they came laughing through the doorway, stamping raindrops from their shoes. A volley of rapid Spanish greeted them. Carlos sighed. "English, please, Elena. You must become proficient in English if you are to be a good American citizen." He patted her cheek in a comradely fashion. "Is it not so?" he asked.

Elena shrugged her shoulders, her dark eyes glistening. "You are late," she shot at Ariana. "And you have much to learn before you will be of use here."

Ariana saw Carlos smother an impatient retort. "I'll see you both at lunch," he reminded them. "You take your hour first, my little firecracker. Ariana will come after you, then she can see a part of Freddy's parrot show before she returns."

Elena made a face, and Carlos took her by the arm and walked her with him to the doorway, speaking to her very seriously. Ariana had to smile when she saw the girl lift her face to Carlos's, inviting his kiss. She turned quickly away, and was inspecting a row of blown-glass miniatures when Elena returned. The Cuban girl was humming contentedly.

"First we will walk together around the shop, and you will see the merchandise. Then I will teach you price codes and how to work the new cash register. It is all electronic," Elena said proudly. "It keeps records within itself."

At ten-thirty Elena stepped back and admitted grudgingly that her new assistant learned rapidly. "After coffee," she said, "you will take your turn dusting. Everything must be clean and tidy every day. Carlos insists upon that."

Elena poured two cups of dark, richly brewed coffee and asked curiously, "How do you know Mr. Ferguson?"

Briefly, Ariana explained. "The coffee was delicious," she said then, putting down her empty cup. "I'll start the dusting, shall I?"

She had finished her share of the chores before their first customers wandered in. "A tour bus," Elena whispered. "Fortunately the rain has ceased and their trip will not be spoiled." With bright smiles of welcome, both girls moved forward to the groups, inviting them to browse as they wished, helping those whose minds were already made up to choose gaily decorated T-shirts, books about parrots, and souvenir bracelets or spoons of sterling silver.

Elena gave Ariana a frosty smile as the last of the tourists drifted out of the shop to begin the tours of the gardens. "You still have much to learn, but I am pleased with things so far. With time you will make a good saleslady."

Ariana beamed. "You're a good teacher."

Elena shot a quick glance in her direction, but met only a friendly smile. "Don't forget to punch in your employee number each time you use the cash register," she reminded her as she left for lunch. "And let us see now if you are just as good at keeping your hands off my property."

She flounced past Freddy, who was just coming in. He grinned cheekily at Ariana. "Fair warning," he said to her.

"Did she think I might steal something while she was at lunch or was that a reference to Carlos?" Ariana asked indignantly.

Freddy's grin grew wider. "You are a pretty lady, Radnor. Doesn't that answer your question?" He told her, "Never fear, Carlos can handle Elena."

"She doesn't like me. She really doesn't. Would it help if I told her I was off men for life?"

Freddy's lips twitched. "You joke. Anyway, it is good for that one to have some competition." He picked up a glass figurine of a parrot and examined it with interest, his large hands gentle on the fragile piece.

"Does—ah—does Carlos return her affection?"

Freddy answered gravely, "Who knows what is in Carlos's mind? He is deep, that one." He placed the glass bird carefully back on the velvet tray. "I came to ask you to visit Pete with me when you have had your lunch."

"Wonderful! I'd like that. Is his leg healing?"

Freddy's merry face sobered. He lifted both hands in a Latin gesture. "Who knows? Carlos wants you to see some of the one-thirty show, too. Part of your indoctrination period, he says."

"How kind. Freddy, thank you."

"Think you can find the way?"

"Down to Pete's cage? Indeed I can."

The smile was back on his broad face. "See you, pretty lady," he said, bowing extravagantly to a little gray-haired woman hesitating in the doorway.

Ariana sold the woman souvenir T-shirts for her six

grandchildren and sighed with relief when the register behaved properly. She counted out the customer's change, explaining that it was her first day of work.

"You're doing beautifully." The woman smiled and patted her hand. "It's nice to see a happy face."

And she *was* happy, Ariana realized. Colorado seemed a long time ago.

She waved to Mr. Ferguson as she left the lounge on her way to see Pete, then walked briskly down the Allamanda Trail, turning off to take the shortcut through the blue garden Mr. Ferguson had named "Lavender's Blue," and on past the orchid slathouses, where Armando Rivas was at work. "Hi," she greeted him, bending over to touch butterfly-like ruby-pink *Phalaenopsis* blooms with a careful hand.

"Mmm, gorgeous things," she breathed. "Do they have a name? They are orchids, aren't they?"

"Yes, orchids. This is my favorite dark pink, the 'Roseheart.' Stewart's out in San Gabriel hybridized this one, Ariana. It has the remarkable German 'Zipperose' in its lineage. You want one?" Armando asked her with his gentle courtesy, detaching a single bloom.

He smiled at her pleasure. "You wear in your hair—like this." His work-stained fingers fastened the flower above her right ear.

Freddy laughed when he saw it there. "Elena will scalp you for sure," he warned. "It means you are unmarried, you know. And looking . . . on the prowl."

She denied it vehemently. "Men!" she sniffed. "Always thinking they're irresistible."

"Hey," Freddy complained, "present company excluded?"

She gave him a rueful glance. "You and Pete. And speaking of Pete?"

"Come and see for yourself," Freddy invited, his face showing his concern.

The African Grey was hunched down at the bottom of his cage. "Hello, Pete," the trainer greeted him.

"Hello, Freddy."

"Here's Radnor come to see you," Freddy said, putting his arm around Ariana and drawing her closer. "Give him this slice of apple," he said in a low voice to her.

Pete accepted the fruit. "Hello, Radnor," prompted Freddy. The parrot gazed mournfully at him.

Freddy opened the cage and lightly stroked the ash-gray feathers. "He's really low. I'm sure worried about him. Talk to him, Ariana. He likes you, I can tell."

Ariana slowly lifted her hand and gently stroked the bird's feathered back. "Hello, Pete," she repeated in a soft voice.

The bird looked at her. "Hello, Radnor," prompted Freddy. Pete hung his head.

"The leg is healing," Freddy explained as they walked away. "A few more days and it should be good as new, but Pete's lost confidence in himself, I'm afraid. Too bad—he's been one of our best talkers, too. At least he's still eating. If he goes off his food, we are in real trouble."

At the thatched-roof building where he and Ken Smith put on their parrot show there were already some spectators on the three tiers of circular benches, waiting for the start of the Paradise Parade. Freddy found her a seat near the exit and went down to join Ken at the table they used as a stage.

Ariana was not too surprised when Carlos slipped into the seat beside her just as a recording of drums and a bugle sounded reveille to open the show. Up a tiny flagpole went a miniature Old Glory with the Blue and Gold Macaw, Milton, standing at attention with one wing slightly raised.

In the thirty minutes that followed, Ariana watched trained macaws, parrots, and cockatoos present acts that included a brief basketball game, roller-skating, a counting game with bell ringing, and some 'IQ' testing by means of boards onto which the birds placed matching colored rings. Between each act a green and blue parrot poised on a tall perch at one end of the stage would lift a foot and shake it at the audience while he shouted "Good-bye!"

"No, no, Dryden. Not yet," Freddy chided him each time.

Carlos whispered to her, "That's Mr. Ferguson's old Blue Crowned Amazon parrot. He's blind in one eye—cataract."

"It can't be fixed?"

"No cure known yet. The bird is forty-six. We're just hoping the other eye remains healthy."

Ariana stole a glance at her wristwatch. "I should go. It's after two."

Carlos shook his head abruptly. "I want you to see the whole performance. It's important for you to know what is going on in the various aspects of Paradise." His dark eyes held her own. "Do not fret. Elena knows where you are."

She said coolly, "I'll bet." She turned her attention to the long table before them where Freddy was playing a highly modified game of poker with Keats, the Scarlet Macaw.

"Keats claims he's the winner with a Full House, folks," Freddy announced over the microphone. "That beats my Two Pairs, for sure. Let's see," the trainer said. "I'll hold up his cards, and Keats will ring the bell to let you know what he was holding. All right, Keats, what have you got?"

Freddy picked up the oversized cards and held them up for the audience to see. "Three threes and two fours. A Full House. Keats wins."

The audience clapped vigorously. Keats stepped up on Freddy's hand and reached for the bell cord with his beak. "Show 'em you know a three," ordered Freddy, and Keats rang the bell three times. The trainer and the performer then repeated the action for the four.

"Good-bye, good-bye," called the Blue Crowned Amazon.

"Not yet, Dryden," groaned Freddy.

"Notice the birds get a food reward each time?" Carlos asked. "Freddy slips it to them so adroitly that most of the people here never realize it's happened. Usually it's a peanut."

"A reinforcement for desired behavior, isn't it?"

"Exactly that. Freddy and Ken have had to change this end act. It used to be Pete, singing some bars of 'Moon over Miami' against a backdrop curtain of stars with old Milton pulling a cord attached to a big yellow moon that 'floated' by. But you know what's happened to Pete—" His voice dropped. "Here's the last act. Keep an eye on Dryden, he's quite a clown."

Ken Smith requested that a lady from the audience step down and assist them in the last act. "Have I a volunteer? How about you?"

An attractive Chinese girl in the second tier of benches nodded shyly and came gracefully forward. "Oh, a pretty lady," Ken said. "Isn't she a pretty lady, Byron?" he asked a Sulfur Crested Cockatoo perched nearby.

The snow-white bird with the flamboyant crest cocked his head for a moment, then Byron's loud, appreciative whistle rent the air. The audience rocked with laughter. "Good-bye! Good-bye!" called Dryden.

Freddy was annoyed. "No, Dryden. Please, not yet!" He walked over to the perch where a pair of gorgeous blue macaws waited patiently. "These beauties are Hyacinthines, folks," Freddy said. "Some of the rarest, most magnificent birds that exist. Expensive, too! This one's Browning, Robert of course," he said, inviting the blue macaw to perch on his arm. "His mate is Barrett, last name of Elizabeth." He lowered Browning to the table. "Ken has an orchid for the lady, Browning. Please take the flower to the pretty lady."

The Hyacinthine picked up the orchid in his beak, shuffled along the table and deposited the flower in front of the visitor. The girl thanked the bird sweetly, and while Ken returned the macaw to the perch by its mate, Freddy expressed their gratitude to the audience for its kind attention and friendly appreciation.

"And now—at last! It's Dryden's turn to bid all you good people our fond farewell," Freddy announced, pointing to the Amazon parrot while Ken began lining up all the performers in a more or less orderly row on the table to take their bows.

Dryden stared at the trainer. Freddy mopped his brow. "And now—at last! It's Dryden's turn," he repeated loudly. "Dryden, you're on!"

"Hello!" chirped Dryden, happily waving one foot to the amused crowd. "Hello, hello, hello."

"So your first week went well," Meg commented, putting the finishing touches on the cake she was frosting that Saturday morning. "I'm glad about that. We've missed seeing you around, though."

Ariana leaned over from the tall kitchen stool and scooped a fingertip of icing from the bowl. "Mmm, *real* boiled frosting. You spoil that man."

"They're worth it, both of them. Sebastian and Luke. You're up early, aren't you? I would have thought you'd sleep late, this one morning you're not off to work."

Ariana stretched lazily. "I've missed the beach. It's rather special just at sunrise."

The long stretches of white sand were rinsed clean of footprints then, and the sea was dawn-quiet blue. She liked to walk barefooted along the shore at that time, with small sandpipers running on ahead of her and the noisy gulls circling in the pale, rose-streaked sky above.

Meg poured coffee into moss-green mugs. "Breakfast, honey? You haven't eaten yet, have you? Sebastian's been in New York the last four days. He just came back late yesterday. He'll want to see you, too."

Ariana's heart turned over. So he'd been away. She *had* wondered, after that last night together, why he hadn't come—or telephoned—

She saw Meg watching her, waiting for an answer. "Thank you, yes, if it's just whatever you were going to have and no fussing."

Meg pulled a pan of freshly-baked pecan breakfast rolls from the oven. "Sticky buns. No fuss," she remarked. "Besides, you're practically one of the family."

"Speaking of family," Ariana laughed, "mine's enlarged by one, as of last night. Pete's living with me for a while."

"Pete?" drawled Seb from the doorway. "I thought the name was Ron."

She stared at him, seeing the anger there, knowing she was more than halfway in love with this man. And knowing it wasn't wise, that it was asking again to be hurt. "Pete's an African Grey, a trained, tamed parrot," she said lightly. "He's been injured, and he started to go off his food. He likes me, so he's come home with me to convalesce a while." She looked right past him, out Meg's kitchen window. "Jumping to conclusions is a risky exercise."

"Sorry," he said, and it rasped as if the word came through his teeth.

Meg put plates down on moss-green, woven place mats. "Sounds as if you both need food in your stomachs." She put the coffee within reach, placed cream and demerara sugar on the table, and left the kitchen.

Seb reached for a sticky bun. "I said I was sorry." There was a calculating look in his eyes. "Or are you angry at me because I've been away and didn't call you?"

"Oh, have you been away?" she asked sweetly, mischief brimming in brown eyes.

His eyebrows rose. "Then you haven't missed me?" His chair scraped back.

She stood up quickly, but his arm caught her around the waist, hauling her close to him. "Don't tease me, woman," he said thickly. "It's too early in the morning. We should be in bed."

She opened her mouth to protest, twisting in his arms, but his hand thrust deep into her hair and his lips came down to hers. "Say you missed me," he muttered, tracing the line of eyebrow and cheek with little kisses. "Say it!"

"Why should I lie?" she admitted shakily. "Yes, I missed you, but—"

He lifted her into his arms and deposited her back in the chair, a satisfied look in his blue eyes. "Eat your breakfast," he directed calmly, a little twist of amusement on his lips when he saw her expression. "I missed you, too," he said, taking a third roll. "Now tell me what's wrong with—Pete, was it?"

"Pete. Short for Petrarch, the great Italian poet, of course." She ignored his astounded look. "Pete broke a leg, and it's healed all right, Seb, but he's gone all melancholy and won't sing."

"Sing?" Seb's lips twitched.

"Yes, 'Moon over Miami'—remember that old song?"

He remembered. "Talks, too, I suppose?"

She frowned. "Like crazy, they tell me. But he has to build up his self-esteem again. That's why he's living with me."

"Of course," Seb said, not quite hiding the smile behind the mug of coffee. "Come out with me tonight?"

The invitation caught her unawares. "Well—" she began, thinking fast.

"It's time you met people," he said smoothly. "Wear something pretty. It's sort of a party."

"Near here?" she asked, thinking of the golf cart. "We could use my VW, or do you have a car?" She hadn't seen one, and she wasn't at all sure he'd even fit in the little car with the white daisy painted on the door.

Seb's smile was wry. "I—er—have a car. Seven-thirty all right?"

It seemed a little early for a party, but she nodded. "I'll be ready."

*

He was right on time, and he whistled appreciatively as she opened the door, dressed in a long, white jersey sheath. "Nice," he told her. "Luke sent you this," he said, bending down to fasten a small white *Cattleya* orchid just above her ear. "Ready? Better bring a wrap."

She had a bronze-pink stole, feather-light and the exact match of the enamel on her toenails. And then it was her turn to whistle, for the car at the end of her flagstone path was a low-slung, dark blue sports car. "A Lancia?" she gasped, eyeing the Pininfarina-styled body.

He nodded. "The Zagato."

She patted the painted daisy as they walked past her small car. "Don't be jealous, I like you too," she assured it. "You're both very snazzy numbers." She sat quietly in the leather bucket seat, wondering how Seb could afford a luxury item like this, and sick with the certainty that she knew how. They listened to the music from the FM radio as the Zagato traveled south. An hour later she stirred and asked, "Miami?"

"A bit beyond," he responded politely. Somewhat later the car swept silently to a halt before the elaborate entrance of an exclusive Coral Gables residential hotel.

"Good evening, sir," the doorman greeted Seb, opening Ariana's door with a little flourish.

"Evening, Pat," Seb responded, casually nodding to the car boy who was sliding into the driver's seat. "Shall we go in?" he asked Ariana.

The dark-haired woman was on the far side of the large room they entered, part of a circle of laughing, talking people. Ariana recognized her at once. "Something wrong?" Seb asked, looking down.

The young woman had seen them now and crossed to greet them. "Seb, how nice. You made it home in time for

my party." She held out both her hands. "Hello," she said
to Ariana. "You're new, aren't you?"

"Antonia Pascale, our hostess—Ariana Radnor," Seb
murmured.

"Call me Tony." She winked at Seb. "A pretty one," she
said pertly.

Seb's eyes narrowed.

Ariana held her head high and just smiled. Emma
French would have recognized the poise and applauded.
Tony Pascale took each of them by an arm and steered
them around the room, performing casual introductions.
These were the important people of Tony's world—the
men and women of big business and high finance, the
judges and physicians and college presidents, the ones
with the private jets and white-water yachts, the diamond
bracelets and designer frocks.

Everyone knew Seb, it seemed. And when Ariana was
introduced, they murmured polite little nothings and
smiled at her cordially. They looked, all of them, as if the
world was their oyster—and it probably was, Ariana
thought.

Tony murmured, "Judge Dalton has been asking for
you, Seb. He's in the study; just don't dare to spend all
night tucked away with him. I'll take care of Ariana while
you're away."

"If you would show me where I might comb my hair?"
Ariana asked. "It was a bit breezy in the Lancia."

She could feel Tony looking her over as she ran a comb
through her fair hair. They were alone in the attractive
apricot- and lemon-colored powder room on the main
floor of the split-level suite. "Have you known Seb long?"
Tony asked.

Ariana applied lip gloss with a light touch. "Sixteen
years."

"My word!" The dark-haired woman was amazed. "I
had no idea."

Ariana smiled innocently into the mirror, her eyes on

Tony. "Wasn't it nice that Seb got back from Chicago in time for us to come to your party?"

Tony blinked. "Chicago? Oh, yes, wonderful," she agreed, hesitating only a moment. "Yes, indeed it was."

And so much for the New York trip, Ariana decided. She kept her smile as they returned to the party, but she was shaken inside.

"My dear," sighed Tony, "I must greet some new arrivals. Will you be all right for just a teeny while? Get Drake to get you a drink."

Ariana drifted around the room, joining little groups for brief intervals, talking easily with the people she met. She danced with a delightful older man, drank champagne with a too-friendly younger one. She watched, listened, and found herself enjoying the evening.

A buffet supper was starting to be served, and when she twirled around, looking for Seb, her elbow touched a man who was standing nearby watching her. She turned to apologize, and her eyes met the tall, fair-haired man she'd last seen in Seb's living room at the Court.

"Hello," he said, and the word held the same two-level intonation as Byron's long whistle. "Who are you?"

She told him, "If I thought you knew Emily Dickinson I'd say 'I'm Nobody! Who are you?' but you're apt to be Somebody, aren't you?" She extended her hand. "Ariana Radnor. I came with Sebastian Farleigh, but we have misplaced each other."

"Good," he said, his gray eyes saying a great deal more. "Drake Lawson. Tony and I are law partners." He considered her thoughtfully. "Supper and—?"

At Montval she had dealt successfully with a hundred men like this one. She smiled sweetly at him and nodded agreeably. The food was delicious and the wine was excellent, but she ate little and turned the wineglass around and around in her hand, listening quietly to the flow of conversation at their table.

Seb came up behind her chair and dropped a kiss on the

top of her head. "I knew it was too good to last," her supper companion complained, rising to his feet, pulling an extra chair into place. "How are you, Sebastian? Was the trip as successful as you hoped?"

Ariana lowered her head and contemplated her wine-glass.

On the way home she asked him, "What does *bubba* mean?"

Seb opened the soft, fold-down back, and balmy air coursed through the car, lifting her hair, cooling her nape. "Used in what way?"

"As in *bubba system.*"

His voice was wary. "Where did you hear that?"

"At the supper table tonight. Judge Dalton came back earlier than you, Seb, and he was talking. Everyone there seemed to know the term."

He said casually, "It's just an old Southern expression, means something like looking after your own little brother—or a friend. Like a small-town cop helping you fix a traffic ticket."

Turning toward him, she said, "It must mean something more than that now, a modern connotation—something to do with drugs?"

Seb said harshly, "It could. It can refer to any basic small-town corruption."

"Explain, please."

He gave her a quick glance. "Illegal operations—and in them the powers-that-be protect their own, from the top drawer down. The system endures because of greed."

She thought about that. "You mean, something's going on, something illegal, and it's known to be going on, but top men in the judiciary are part of this bubba system, and some lawyers, too, and then some of the police, and on and on down the line to the smallest of the operators, each getting his share of the cut?"

"Something like that," Seb agreed.

Ariana smiled bitterly. "Tell me again, why can't it be stopped? And it's not just small-town anymore, is it?"

"Corruption feeds on itself and spreads. The bubba system long ago left the small town for the big city. It could be stopped except for two factors—greed and fear."

They were almost home. She leaned back and studied his profile. "Beautiful car," she said after a few moments' silence. "How long have you had it?"

"Six months."

That figured.

"Aren't you inviting me in for coffee?" He fitted her key in the lock and smiled down at her.

She smiled back. There were some things she wanted to ask this man, and the wine had made her brave. "The real kind," she promised. "No instant coffee tonight."

They stood on the deck, comfortably close, watching the ocean while the coffee perked. Tense inside, Ariana then fixed the tray and brought it into the living room, where Seb sank down on the long sofa and patted the cushion beside him.

"Sit by me," he ordered bluntly. "I want to talk to you."

She gave him a direct look. "I want to talk to you, too. And I'm first. Why did you take me to the party tonight, Seb? I think I know, but I want you to tell me."

He leaned over and put the Ming Rose coffee cup and saucer on the end table. "You're a stubborn woman, Ariana Radnor." The wide shoulders shrugged. "I wish I knew what you were thinking."

She could play this game, too. "You mean you wish you knew how much I know."

His smile was cool. Leaning over, his lips brushed her cheek, and her pulse leaped. "A different fragrance tonight, isn't it?"

She nodded. "Nice," he offered, "but not quite the staying power of *Je Reviens,* I would say, wouldn't you?"

Uneasily, she asked him: "You knew I was out on the terrace that night, didn't you?"

He watched her for a moment, an uncertain expression on his face, and when he spoke his voice was guarded. "I suspected that it was you. There was a—a special fragrance on the night air. I recognized your perfume, so I lit my pipe and the tobacco smoke quite covered up your tracks."

She forced herself to say it. "That sounds as if it would have been, at the least, embarrassing, and at the most, dangerous, for me, yet you kept your friends from knowing. You protected me. Why?"

He lifted his dark head and looked at her. "I think you know."

He had his arms around her, pulling her close to him, and she closed her eyes. His mouth moved over her lips, slowly, softly, coaxingly. "Kiss me, darling," he murmured unevenly, his fingers stroking her flushed cheek, her bright hair. His heart was pounding against her breasts, and she felt the echo of it flood through her body, warming it with treacherous fire.

With a little shiver she put both hands against his chest and pushed. "No," she cried out, her voice sword-sharp with the pain of separation.

His arms dropped instantly from her. "No?" His smile was sardonic now.

"Seb, please—" She placed her small hand lightly on his clenched one. "If you make love to me now, I shall always think it was only to distract me."

A flush stained his face. A muffled exclamation escaped his lips and he said flatly, "Is there more coffee?"

She kicked off her sandals and walked to the kitchen in her bare feet. When she returned with the percolator, he was standing by the french windows, staring out into the night, his hands thrust deep into trouser pockets. Carelessly discarded on the nearest lounge chair were his suit jacket and tie.

"All right," he said, turning to her. "We'll talk."

"Tell me first why you took me to Tony's party tonight."

Some of the tension seemed to go out of his muscles. "I had to make certain if you'd been on the terrace that night or not," he said ruefully, dropping down on the sofa again. "Before I could decide on my next step, I first had to know that. One look at your face when you saw Tony tonight and I had my answer."

"Does it matter? That I was there?" Her fingers tightened on the coffee cup. With a mounting sense of alarm she asked, "What do you mean—decide on the next step?"

He closed his eyes wearily, leaning his head back. "It matters, very much. But I can handle it, keep you safe, if no one else on God's earth knows. Tell me, how much did you overhear that night?"

She looked at him. "Not much. But it's drugs, isn't it, Seb? You've gotten involved with illicit drugs." She said contemptuously, "How could you? You—a physician—mixed up with the filthy stuff."

His face hardened into ice. "We'll skip the incriminations, shall we, and concentrate instead on saving your life? I've got to think this out."

"I'm glad I didn't fall in love with you," she cried out. "Almost—almost I did, Seb. Thank God I didn't. I couldn't stand myself if I loved you, Sebastian Farleigh."

He reached for her, kissing away the tears that were running down her face, holding her close to him while his hand gently rubbed the nape of her neck. "Hush. Hush, darling—let me think this through. There's not much time—"

"Less than three weeks, right?" Brown eyes sparkled with anger. She pulled herself from his arms, her hand flying out and striking his cheek. "You coward! You despicable coward! Or is it the greed you spoke of earlier tonight? What's your cut, Seb? Nine million dollars? What will you buy with your share of the grief and broken lives and ruined genetic patterns in young bodies—a new Lancia Zagato? Your own Learjet? A villa in France?"

He seized her shoulders and shook her, anger glittering

in blue eyes. "Damn you for a stubborn creature, Ariana. Stop shouting at me and let me think, or do you want your sandals and a beach towel to be found tomorrow morning at the ocean's edge, and not a trace of you?"

He saw her ashen, frightened face and swore. "Oh, my darling, I'm sorry—I wouldn't hurt you, I swear it, but this is a hazardous game, and I can't vouch for the others."

"A game? Played by scum," she said shakily. "Scum, Seb —nothing else, and you're scum, too, if you're part of it."

He crossed to the desk and poured himself a whisky. "How did you get such a close inkling of the time factor?" he asked.

"It didn't take great brains to realize you wanted me anywhere but staying on the grounds of the Court. You and all those job offers down in Miami! It seemed only reasonable to assume that I was getting in the way of something. 'Stay two weeks, stay three weeks,' you kept saying, 'and *then* be on your way.' "

"And the plastic envelopes tipped you off to what it was all about?" he drawled. "I was afraid of that."

"That—and some other things."

He saw her glance at the telephone, and he shook his head. "Don't try, darling. This is much too complicated. I want you to sit down here by me and just listen. Just listen, will you do that?"

"Have I a choice?"

He said regretfully, "Not any more." He put a glass of sherry in her cold hands. "Try to relax," he urged. "You have no idea how much I need your help now."

Nausea stirred within her. "I wouldn't help run drugs if my life depended on it."

"And it just well might," he said with a dark glance. "Yours. Mine. Luke's, Meg's; and about ten others could get hurt as well if I don't handle this just right."

"I don't believe you. Meg and Luke would never be involved with drugs."

"Believe me. They'd be two of the innocent ones to die

when the men moved in to get me. Ariana," he said seriously, "if I promised you on my honor that this is the last time, ever, for me—no, wait, let me finish—the *last* time, would you help me?"

"How?"

"By your silence. That's all I'm asking of you. I need time. Will you do that for me—be absolutely silent about all this?"

Her mind was racing ahead. This was utter madness. She said unhappily, "Oh, Seb, how can I trust you?"

He was pacing the living room floor now, his face pale beneath the tan, his eyes on her bent head. He took a step toward her and sighed as she shrank back against the sofa cushions. "I love you. I've fallen deeply in love with you," he said huskily. "God, Ariana, if something should happen to you—" His eyes held hers. "I swear to you on the love I have for you that I'm getting out of this involvement with drugs."

For a moment happiness flooded through her like a river, lifting her heart. She spoke and her voice was cool. "Is this resolution of yours a recent one, Seb?"

"No," he admitted. "Believe it or not, but I had already made some plans to get out before you ever came. Such a stubborn one you are, darling. I tried so hard to get you out of here before you might be hurt, before your presence here somehow harmed my chances, but—"

"Don't tell me," she begged. "Don't tell me any more. I know too much for my conscience as it is." There goes peace of mind, she thought uneasily, knowing herself to be seven kinds of a fool. She told him, "All right, Seb, I have your word of honor that if I keep silent now you will extricate yourself from this involvement—at whatever personal cost and risk?"

He lowered his head. "You have my word."

She was having difficulty keeping her voice steady. "There's one thing more I'll ask of you: you will never, from this moment forward, accept a single dollar as a cut, share, payment, or portion of this or any other drug scheme."

Seb looked as if she had kicked him in the gut. "You should have been a lawyer," he said dryly. "But yes, you have my word on that, too."

"Then tell me, please, what to do to help you." She looked shyly at him. "I'll do anything, Seb—anything— just so it's not illegal."

"Nothing."

"You mean, do nothing at all?"

"Absolutely nothing. Go on with your job at Paradise, your life here, as if nothing is different. That's vital, darling. There might be someone watching you, I don't know. I don't think anyone's caught on to you, but I know their technique. Ask no questions, behave toward me just as you've always done. Speak to no one about any of this. No one at all. Not Meg. Not Luke. Nobody." His eyes were troubled. "Think you can do this, darling? For three, maybe four, perhaps fewer weeks? Your safety depends on it. If you can't, or if you're afraid you might slip, tell me now and I'll get you out of here tonight—perhaps back to Colorado? That would seem natural."

She told him fiercely, "No one's going to make me run from you."

He crossed the room in rapid strides and caught her to him, holding her close in his arms with his cool cheek pressed against her hair. "Darling," he said hoarsely. "God, darling, let me kiss you."

She lifted her face to him and his hands moved over her body, slowly, delighting her while their mouths clung. "Do you love me?" he asked her, his lips against her own. "Say you love me, Ariana."

She felt his heart beat, heard his ragged breathing, and her body sang. "I love you," she said quietly. "I've never been in love like this before, never—"

His hands were tender, touching her young breasts; his arms possessive as he carried her to her bed. She lay in his arms there, her head against the hollow near his shoulder, while his lips drifted down her cheek, her throat, and to the gentle curving of her breasts.

"I want you—I need you, darling—darling, darling, if I stay, you'll have to let me love you—" he groaned. "And I want to stay, I want to, woman—"

"Seb," she whispered lovingly, touching his hair, feeling the crispness of it in her fingertips. "Seb, it's the first time . . . ever . . ."

For a long moment he lay still, then his hand tenderly turned her face to his. "I'm going to be your lover, dear heart—but not tonight." He held her close to him, comfortingly close. "Tonight is for promises," he said, his face hidden in her fragrant hair. "We'll work out our tomorrows."

He raised himself on one elbow to look down at her. "Oh, my love—remember what I've said tonight. You know nothing. You say nothing."

Her hair lay spread in a golden tangle on the pillow. "I'll remember," she promised him. But there was something else to ask, too. "Seb, how will I know when this is over? All over?"

He looked down at her where she lay, her brown eyes anxious, her bare shoulders honey-gold against the white pillow. Slowly, tenderly, he kissed her goodnight. "You'll know, small one," he promised quietly. "I'll ask you to marry me then, that's how you'll know."

CHAPTER 9

It was going to be a wonderful day. Ariana awakened, her mind almost at peace and her heart full of happiness. She sang as she showered and dressed, and ran lightheartedly down the path to reach her car and start off for work.

Everything was going to be all right!

September was passing in golden days of incredible beauty. Day after day the tropical skies were blue.

Paradise was a triumph of color. With Mr. Ferguson as her guide, Ariana often spent part of her lunch hours now, sitting quietly in the special garden named "White on White," while he identified for her the creamy blossoms of the fragrant *Plumeria* trees under which they sat, and the spectacular white-laden branches of the leathery oleander bushes, with low-growing drifts of white *Pentas* and little *Vinca roseas* at their bases. He helped her find, tucked back in the cooler shade, a ground-cover mass of fragile white rain lilies, the *Zephyranthes*.

Slender vines of stephanotis climbed skyward here, their fragrant white flowers reminiscent of bridal bouquets. Pale drifts of pure white *Thunbergia grandiflora* and rare white *Antigonon* cascaded from the tall pines in festoons of dainty loveliness, and Armando's baskets of showy white *Cattleya* orchids delighted every eye.

The months would bring changes in the plants that bloomed, of course, according to their flowering season, but the basic color schemes in the five gardens remained. Ariana wondered if she would ever learn all the names.

Her favorite place was the tranquil garden they called "Blossomtime." Here the flowers of trees, shrubs, and vines were always in shades of pink and rose, and now in September the secluded enclosure held all the loveliness of northern apple orchards in springtime bloom.

"Come and see it, please," Ariana begged Luke. In a day or two, to please her, Luke arrived and spent hours with Armando and Mr. Ferguson, walking also through "Mixed Palette" and "Lavender's Blue," and taking home with him treasured cuttings from Armando's new blush rose crape myrtle and some seeds of *Peltophorum*, the spectacular yellow *Flamboyant* tree.

Seb met Ariana on the beach that night. Eight days had passed since Tony's party, and when he walked her back to La Casita, she could see signs of strain beneath his shadowed eyes.

"You're losing weight," he said worriedly, his hand lingering on her cheek. "Aren't you sleeping nights?"

She reached for his hand. "No news?" she asked quietly, and the frown on his face told her instantly that she had touched the forbidden topic.

"Come here, darling," he muttered, enfolding her within his arms. "Let me kiss you."

Strong hands caressed her back, and his mouth parted her lips. She yielded to him, finding joy in the warmth of his body, in the sweetness of the embrace.

Suddenly she felt him stiffen, then lift his head. From off shore came the sound of powerful motors, pulsing closer. "What is it?" she asked.

His face was silent, listening. "Lock your doors after me," he warned her in a low voice. "And don't come out again tonight—not even out onto the deck. Promise?" He put a hand under her chin, searching her face. Shakily she nodded, and with a quick hard kiss on her lips he was gone.

That night she forced herself to prepare a proper meal of broiled steak and a tossed salad, and she sat at the cherry-wood table until every crumb had vanished. Finally she rose, weary all the way through her body, to prepare for bed.

She wakened early from a restless night and spent the extra time working with Pete, caring for his needs of food and water, and practicing word phrases with him. His voice was soft and clear, not harsh like so many of the other birds. It even, she admitted only to herself, sounded very much like a human voice.

"Don't kid yourself that Pete's talking to you like another human being," Freddy had warned her early on. "If a trained bird talks, it's either imitative speech when he mimics the trainer's words, or it's conditioned response as he replies to his trainer's cue words with a learned answer. He's not really *talking* to you, not with reasoned responses, remember."

But as Pete learned to accept Ariana, his melancholy gradually departed, and she had found his vocabulary to be downright phenomenal. She went about her tasks that morning with a heavy heart, worrying about Seb as she cleaned Pete's cage and ran through his repertoire with him.

Pete climbed from her hand to her left shoulder after the vocabulary exercises were completed. This was something new and deserved a special treat. She talked to the bird, gently stroking its throat, then offered a peanut.

He stayed on her shoulder as she washed the breakfast dishes and even when she started to make the bed. "Well, good for you, Pete," she told him, greatly encouraged. At least something was turning out right on this bright September morning.

Ariana hummed as she straightened the crocheted coverlet and fluffed up the pillows. Suddenly she stopped, turned her head to the left, and listened.

Pete was singing the first six syllables of his theme song!

Ariana could hardly wait to get to work and tell Freddy. "Isn't it wonderful? He sounds almost real, too—I mean he sounds just like a person crooning the 'Moon over Miami' phrase."

The trainer hugged her. "I knew he'd do it for you if he did it for anyone, Radnor. Let's celebrate tonight!"

"Sorry, no dates. I won't go out with you, Freddy, but you simply have to hear Pete perform. Come to supper at my place—seven o'clock, okay?"

His smile was wry. "Okay, but what's this 'no dates' business?" His dark eyes flashed, and she was almost tempted to withdraw the invitation.

All that day she avoided him by skipping lunch at the lounge and working steadily through her usual break. It was one of their busiest days so far, with tour groups from Germany and Holland there in the morning, and two chartered busloads of French tourists arriving in the afternoon. Ariana's pleasant voice could be heard chatting helpfully in French or German, and Elena added her sincere thanks to Carlos's when the last bus pulled away from Paradise.

"Is something wrong, Carlos? You look—strained," Ariana said. "It's not Mr. Ferguson; he's not ill, is he?"

"We've lost some birds," he told the two girls. "Why don't you drop by the office this afternoon before you leave, Ariana? Cheer him up a little. He's fretting also about Hurricane Christine maybe heading our way after all. Puerto Rico's taken quite a pounding, and the latest advisory warns that it's somewhat more westerly now."

Ariana found her elderly friend sitting on the office sofa, his sad eyes following Carlos's figure as the manager moved about outside, tending to the closing-up chores that were his special responsibility.

"Ariana," Mr. Ferguson said shakily, "something's happening here, lassie. Something's wrong."

She caught his cold hands, holding them in her own warm ones, speaking soothingly to him. "Were they the new cockatoo babies? Did they get suddenly sick?"

"The Hyacinthines, the mated pair."

"Not Browning and Barrett!" That beautiful, expensive pair of macaws.

Mr. Ferguson nodded mournfully. "Stolen from us, like as not. Carlos knows something, I can tell. He's not talking, though. Says the less publicity the better."

"But how?"

She asked Freddy that question, too, when, after his delighted reunion with Pete, they sat down to a supper of herb toast, a huge shrimp salad, and chocolate cake. Meg had brought the cake over before she left for West Palm when she heard Ariana was having company.

"How could anyone steal two large birds like those macaws? And the birds wouldn't go quietly, would they? Someone must have seen or heard something."

"I'd guess there was some inside help." Freddy frowned. "We've been asked not to discuss it," he said brusquely. "But I damn well wish I knew what Carlos has gotten into."

"Carlos?" she asked, astonished. "You're surely not thinking that Carlos had anything to do with it. That man lives and breathes for Paradise."

"Exactly that." He smiled, and his smile was not one of amusement. "He *wants* Paradise, Ariana. But he could never afford to buy it."

"Call the cops!" Pete shouted from his cage in the living room. "Hello, Freddy! Call the cops!"

"Quiet down, you old bastard, I want to talk to the pretty lady." Freddy fed the bird a crumb of cake. "He looks great, Ariana. I'd like to get him back in the show soon."

"I wish he'd sing for you. Maybe if I put him on my shoulder and hummed to him?" She placed her coffee cup down on the end table and turned toward the cage.

Freddy stepped in front and caught her in his arms. "You're very beautiful, pretty lady," he murmured, his admiring eyes drifting over her and fastening on her astonished mouth.

"Let me go, Freddy. I mean it."

Her protests were silenced under his moist, hungry mouth. Furious now, she frantically twisted free. "And don't dare ever do that again!"

"Call the cops!" Pete cried, and Freddy stepped back with a rueful smile on his handsome face. "Even the bird's against me," he said mournfully. "You're a gorgeous girl, Ariana. You can't blame a man for trying."

"All right!" she said sharply. "And now you know. I'm not up for grabs, remember that. I thought we were friends, Freddy."

He reached into Pete's cage and set the parrot on her left shoulder. "Friends, ha," he scoffed lightly, grinning at her.

With a hand that still shook a little, Ariana soothed the bird, humming softly to it. Loud knocking at the dutch door startled all of them. "Anyone home?" called Seb.

With the parrot still on her shoulder, Ariana went to let him in. "Meg tells me the dessert's served down here," Seb said blandly, a comprehending light in his eyes as he observed her flushed cheeks. "Is Pete okay? What's he doing on your shoulder?"

"Hello," said Pete.

That broke the ice, and the two men sat companionably in the living room, talking about the parrot, while Ariana served cake and coffee, and later, Benedictine.

"There's one thing I still don't know," she said, returning Pete to his cage and rejoining her two guests. "How does one tell them apart, male and female, I mean? The macaws and the parrots all look alike to me."

Freddy smiled, and Ariana hastily retorted, "Don't go giving me any jazzy answer. I'm asking a serious question, Freddy. It isn't in the plumage at all, is it?"

The trainer motioned toward Pete. "No, you usually can't tell by their plumage. An African Grey parrot, the kind Pete is, is specially hard to sex—which is the proper term for differentiating the birds," he said quickly.

"There are some clues though—the male is usually a trifle larger, as Pete is, and the eye shape is slightly different in the female. The droppings can be tested for hormone content, too. But knowing the sex isn't really that important unless you want to breed birds. We've never found any real difference in their ability to talk, and that's their main function at Paradise, you know."

Seb was interested. "The proof of the pudding being a bird's laying an egg, I presume."

That launched Freddy off again on his favorite topic of parrots. "Well, there is a really scientific way to determine a bird's sex early and accurately. We call it 'scoping. It's a simple surgical procedure," he explained, refilling his liqueur glass, "usually always done by a veterinarian. It runs into money, of course, and we've used it rarely at Paradise." He looked over at Ariana. "Browning and Barrett, that mated pair of rare Hyacinthines—Barrett had been 'scoped."

"Laparoscopy," mused Seb, rising to his feet. "Most interesting. But it's past ten and tomorrow's a working day. Why don't I jog on down to the gates, Messina, and lock them after you. Save Ariana a trip." He gave her an amused look, and shook hands with Freddy. "Better listen to the eleven o'clock advisory weather report," he suggested. "It looks as if Christine has changed course again. Towards us."

Freddy leaned back against the doorway watching Ariana. "You're a very lovely girl, Radnor, but if I don't leave pronto, I'll wager he'll be right back to see why."

She made a face at him. "I like you better in your lighthearted moods, Freddy, not the romantic ones. See you tomorrow."

"He'll be back in ten minutes," she decided, thinking of Seb and eager to be with him. She moved gracefully about the living room, clearing dishes and straightening pillows. When he had not returned by the time she had finished the supper dishes, Ariana was disturbed. Surely Seb had taken no offense at her having Freddy over for a light meal, not when he knew about Pete's new progress?

She tried the telephone and got only a busy signal. Meg, probably, she decided, but then remembered that by now Luke and Meg would have left for West Palm Beach for two days so that Luke could finish up with his dentist.

She thought, blushing a little, that perhaps Seb was waiting for her to come to him. Well, why not—She dabbed a bit of *Je Reviens* to her wrists, reached for a flashlight, locked up her house, and was off, hurrying along the now familiar path.

The breeze seemed much stronger now, but it was a glorious night with a star-laden sky. A night for lovers. She heard music, faintly, as she reached the Court, and she moved more slowly up the terrace steps. She had a heavy feeling in her heart, a sensation that all this had happened once before.

She could see right into the room, of course . . . see Seb leaning forward, listening intently, the palms of his hands flat on his knees . . . and the fair-haired man from Tony's party, Drake somebody or other, talking excitedly . . . and Carlos—

Carlos? She stood there, gaping. She bit her lip, hard, to keep from crying out, and then plodded slowly back home again.

She brushed her teeth and washed, then turned out all the lights and crept into her bed. The stars were still bright and there was just that half of a moon in the sky. She sat up against her pillows, looking out through the opened shutters, thinking.

"Trust me," Seb had said. "I pledge you my word." She was so confused. She lay back on her pillows, uneasy and uncertain again, and the tears began, silently at first, so that she heard the sound of the boat's motors, slowly pulsing out of the inlet and then streaking powerfully for white water.

*

The storm began around two o'clock in the morning, with rain lashing at the windows and a heavy surf pounding great breakers high up onto the beach. Ariana wakened, a shiver racing through her body. Pray God that Seb was safely off the water . . . She slipped from the bed and ran to the living room, closing windows all around the little house.

Pete had awakened, too, and was moving uneasily in his cage. Ariana lit several of the lamps, speaking quietly to the bird as she moved about the room. She stood at the window, but it was impossible to see anything at all through the rain-swept glass. She sank down on a chair and flicked on the television set, but the picture was obscured. Almost two o'clock—perhaps there'd be a weather report on the radio's late late news.

Outside, in the darkness of the stormy night, palm fronds whipped and trees bowed branches. "Winds in gusts up to gale force," the newsman acknowledged, "an early effect of Tropical Storm Christine. Christine, gathering new strength as she roared over open water, and upgraded to hurricane status once more, has changed course significantly within the last six hours and is surging northwest at an accelerating rate of twelve miles per hour with 150-mile winds churning the seas over an area three hundred miles in diameter."

Hurricane Christine was a killer of a storm, shifting course erratically. The National Hurricane Center would take no chances: South Floridians awakened on September seventeenth to a 6 A.M. advisory that issued a Hurricane Watch all the way from Key West to the Palm Beaches. If Christine maintained present course, residents were advised, the storm was less than three days away from the Florida coast.

CHAPTER 10

When Ariana awoke again it was nearly seven, and the night's rainstorm was over. A brisk breeze whipped her nightdress about her ankles as she stood on the deck and watched the pale gold-and-pink streaks of early sunshine touch the eastern sky.

The telephone rang as she was dressing, and she reached for the receiver with shaking hands. "Good morning," Meg said briskly. "Just wanted to tell you Luke and I came back early. It looks as if we might get this storm, Ariana—maybe not right on the nose, but within the peripheral high winds."

"Is Seb there?" Ariana asked because she simply had to know. I don't think I can stand two more weeks of this uncertainty, she thought bleakly.

"I think he's in the shower right now," Meg replied. "Want him to call you back when he comes down for breakfast? Oh, I nearly forgot—Luke left a morning paper by your door."

"Thank him for me, please. No, Meg, don't bother Seb —he'll have plenty to do getting ready for Christine."

It was enough, just knowing he was safely home. She could almost hear Meg's mind at work. "Listen, honey," Meg said. "They'll be needing you at Paradise, so you just leave everything at La Casita to us. We're used to this sort of preparation and you're not. You'll be with us for the hurricane itself, of course. If it does come, that is."

"Thank you again," she said, and then it was Seb's voice

in her ear, saying good morning as if nothing had happened the evening before. *Nothing at all.*

"Come over for dinner tonight," he suggested. "Call it a hurricane briefing. I'll pick you up about six-thirty, all right?"

Of course it was all right. Everything was beautifully all right because Seb was home and safe and out of the storm. She refused to let her thoughts go beyond that point.

She fixed toast and coffee, prepared a slice of golden papaya melon, and sat down at the table with the morning newspaper to enjoy her breakfast. She saw the story of the boat chase at once, for it headed the local news. Blood beat at her temples as she read the account.

An attempt had been made last night by federal agents of the Drug Enforcement Administration, in cooperation with state and local police, the Coast Guard, and U.S. Customs, to seize two boatloads of "cocaine cowboys" in action. But the rendezvous signals from the supplier "mother ship" had been confusing, and after a high speed ocean chase one of the two boats sighted had escaped, and the DEA agents seized only the second boat, abandoned in flight. Thirty pounds of pure cocaine and four pounds of heroin, with an estimated street value of thirty-eight million dollars or more, were found aboard the abandoned craft. Illicit drug trafficking, the newspaper reminded its readers, had become a multibillion-dollar business in South Florida. And this was factual evidence.

Ariana folded up the paper. She finished her coffee and pushed aside the toast. Her appetite had vanished.

At Paradise things continued as usual on the surface, but underneath was a different bustle of activity. Visitors strolled the gardens and browsed in the gift shop, but Freddy cut the Paradise Parade shows to just one in the morning and one in the early afternoon.

The grounds crew was pulling down coconuts, pruning limbs near electric wires, and assisting Ken and Freddy in boarding up windows in the birds' night quarters, a concrete building where emergency containers of water now joined the usual sacks of feed stored there. Battery-powered lamps and fans were provided, because electricity invariably failed in the big storms. A tier of bleacher seats was rolled in to hold the bird cages that usually hung in the various gardens. If the storm came, the trainers would stay in the adjacent grounds crew's lounge to care for the birds.

Ariana was given a quick look at the two baby cockatoos when she carried in several hands of bananas and a bag of apples that Florence had sent down. There was still no news of the missing Hyacinthines.

Windows in Mr. Ferguson's house and office were already covered with protective aluminum shutters. The gift shop and the other areas within actual view of the public, however, would be left until last. Ariana stopped at the lounge for a quick cup of coffee with Mr. Ferguson and Florence, and it looked like night in there with the windows all covered.

"Once Hurricane Watch is announced, we do everything in advance that we can," Mr. Ferguson said. "But it's business as usual right up to "Hoist Hurricane Warnings" advisory. And when that comes, lassie, we must take immediate precautions because we have maybe six hours, sometimes much less, to close Paradise, send most of the workers home to care for their own places, and finish whatever still needs to be done."

"But if Christine veers again, then all that preparation is for nothing, isn't it?" Ariana said in a dispirited way.

Florence snorted. "We hope we'll be that lucky. Better to be ready for the big blow and have it sail on elsewhere, than not to be well prepared when it slams into the land."

Mr. Ferguson's gentle eyes met Ariana's warm brown ones. "We won't know about this one until late tomorrow, lassie. Maybe not until very early Friday. We'll just keep listening to the advisories." He sighed. "It will tear up the gardens if it comes. We can't board the gardens up."

He didn't look at all well, Ariana thought. She saw that Florence was watching him closely, too.

It was when she was going back to work from this break that she saw the unusual couple ahead of her. They were walking rather rapidly along Allamanda Trail, arguing in low tones. Ariana noticed them at once because they were so completely different from the usual tourists who strolled slowly along the paths, reading every label and taking pictures of flowers and birds along the way.

This woman was bored silly with Paradise, anyone could see that. Not that the man was much better, Ariana decided. With his linen handkerchief he kept flicking the dust off his highly polished black shoes.

They stopped once, read the descriptive label on the outside of the cage that held a rare Yellow Tailed Black Cockatoo, then walked on, turning off the Trail into "Mixed Palette."

"Armando!" Ariana called softly, seeing the head gardener nearby. "Did you notice that couple? About forty or so, I'd say. The man has a sharp-featured face and the woman with him is wearing three-inch heels. Did you see them?"

Armando carefully lifted down a hanging basket of blue *Cattleya* orchids, the "Sapphire" variety from Stewart's of California. "I see only you, Ariana. What is wrong? Did they speak rudely to you?"

"No." She was filled with uncertainty. "Probably just my imagination, but with the Hyacinthines stolen—"

"You tell Carlos," Armando suggested at once. "Better to be sure."

Of course it was better to be sure. But Carlos? After last night she was no longer certain about Carlos either.

"I'll tell Freddy, he's closer. I'm probably just being silly anyway." She reached up to help lift down a teakwood container of creamy yellow orchids edged in red with rosy-red lips. "Mmm—pretty things. What are these?"

"From Jones and Scully. Their *Brassolaeliacattleya* Melinda Wheeler 'Halcyon.' A really fine yellow, is it not? We bring all the hanging baskets of orchids into Mr. Ferguson's house today. Those plants that are naturalized in the trees must take their chances in the big wind."

She turned away. "I'm crossing my fingers that Christine just blows herself off somewhere into the Atlantic, Armando."

Freddy was setting up for the eleven o'clock Paradise Parade. Ariana ran up to him, pushing her hair back from her face. "This wind!" she exclaimed. "Freddy, there's still no news on the blue macaws, is there? Well, this may be silly of me, but there's the strangest couple here this morning, and I—I sort of wondered—"

Her voice trailed off, for Freddy was watching her through lowered eyelids as he readied the bells and cards and roller skates for the trained bird acts. "Did your watchdog come back after I left last night?" he asked, and there was a bite in his voice.

Ariana flushed. "If you mean Seb, no, he did not." Eagerly, she told him, "You should have heard Pete this morning. Just that one phrase, but he sings it *beautifully!*"

Freddy grinned. "Want to help with the show? Ken won't mind."

"Oh, I'd love to, really I would, but I have to get back to work. I'm late coming in from my break as it is. Freddy, about that couple—I wish you'd take a look at them; they're no bird lovers, or garden fanciers either. He just plain looks evil, all rat-faced, Freddy, and the woman is so bored you can tell it at a glance."

The trainer laughed. "They probably not only look bored, they probably are bored, Ariana. Lots of folk drift in to kill a couple of hours between planes. We're not everybody's cup of tea, girl."

She frowned. "I know, but—"

"You've gone hyper on those Hyacinthines, haven't you?" He studied her thoughtfully. "Tell you what, after the show I'll take a look around. Okay? Better get back to

the gift shop if you're going—it looks like another downpour again."

She heard the start of the reveille record. "Thanks,
Freddy. It looks as if you'll have quite a crowd, doesn't it?
See you later."

But as the first slash of rain struck her face she thought, I
waited just thirty seconds too long. She ducked back under shelter and gave the darkened sky a nervous inspec-
tion. Thank heavens the gift shop wasn't busy. Elena
would be able to handle things alone for another twenty
minutes.

Over her shoulder she could hear the laughter of the
audience as the macaws began the performance. "Good-
bye, good-bye," called Dryden, and Ariana smiled. Soon
Pete would be back with them, too.

She pushed aside the curtain and groped her way to an
empty seat. It was darker than usual in the thatched-roof
building, and Ken had rigged up extra lighting for the
stage area.

The birds seemed nervous today. Probably they sensed
the coming storm, she thought. Freddy was aware of this
feeling, and his deft hands stroked the birds more fre-
quently, calming them with his gentle touch and his familiar voice.

While rain pounded down on the thatch, the audience
enjoyed the show. Dryden's eager attempts to get into the
acts brought waves of laughter each time the bird called
out. Ariana's eyes were accustomed to the dark now, and
she surveyed the crowd. About seventy people—not bad
at all for a stormy day. She saw the couple that had caught
her attention earlier. They were in the second tier of
seats, quite near the entranceway.

Ariana smiled. The woman was yawning. Her companion, though, had his narrow eyes glued to the parrots'
stage.

"Keats claims he's the winner with a Full House, folks,"
Freddy was announcing over the microphone. "That

beats my Two Pairs for sure. Let's see," the trainer said, continuing with his familiar patter. "I'll hold up his cards and Keats will ring the bell to let you know what he was holding. All right, Keats, what have you got?"

Freddy held up the oversized cards for the audience to see. "Three threes and two nines! A Full House! Keats wins!"

Ariana blinked. Nines? Wasn't it always fours at that part? Freddy'd gotten the cards mixed up.

The audience applauded, and Keats stepped up onto Freddy's hand and, as always, reached for the bell cord with his beak. Ariana heard Freddy tell the macaw to "show 'em you know a three," and Keats rang the bell three times.

The act proceeded, but when Freddy called for a nine Keats rang the bell for a four. Poor Keats . . . and poor Freddy, too. He looked quite shattered when he realized what he had done.

"Tell you what, folks," Freddy said, shaking his head. "Keats is half right, anyway, even if he didn't know his two nines. Let's give him a hand," Freddy suggested, slipping the confused Keats his usual food reward. The crowd responded enthusiastically.

"And here's Ken Smith, just back from the front office with the latest advisory on Hurricane Christine," Freddy announced loudly, terminating the applause. "Ken?"

Ariana crouched in her seat, not wanting to move until the audience, and especially her strange couple, had departed. She supposed that even Freddy, who knew the acts backwards and forwards, could make a mistake, but it all seemed a little odd. "Well, blame it on Christine," she muttered half-aloud. "That lady's got us all mixed up."

And Freddy looked so contrite that Ariana determined not to mention the incident. Not to *anyone*.

The last ones out of the thatched hut were her strange couple. The man seemed to be having some difficulty in getting his companion to her feet. She staggered, and

Freddy, fortunately, was near at hand and caught her before she could fall in her three-inch heels.

Ariana slid out behind the curtain and left by the little-used rear exit. One good thing had happened, anyway—Freddy had gotten a real look at the two of them, probably even talked with them a little.

*

As she drove through Hibiscus late that afternoon, Ariana could see the long lines of people in the drug store and the convenience grocery shop. Everyone was out buying candles and canned goods, beer, batteries, and bread, and then hurrying home to begin boarding up their windows.

"Hello, Pete!" Ariana called out as her key turned in the lock and the dutch door swung open.

"Hello, Radnor!"

"Oh, you darling—have you had a good day?" she asked, and the bird promptly responded, "Fair. How was yours?"

Ariana knew this was all conditioned response, but it delighted her every time. "Hey," she suggested, "how about a duet?" Lightheartedly she sang the first bars of "Moon over Miami."

Pete sang along with her for the first few words, then stopped. "Never mind," Ariana consoled him. "One of these days I'm certain you'll get beyond those first six syllables."

Pete crooned softly to her, then stopped and cocked his head to one side. "What's for dinner?" he asked in an inquisitive voice.

Seb grimaced as she told him about it that evening at the Court. Meg was weak with laughter, and even sober Luke had found her conversation with Pete amusing, but Seb's attitude was just the opposite.

As Luke served them cocktails on the terrace, Seb asked, "What good is a trained parrot, may I ask?"

Ariana's eyes filled with amusement. "Oh, come on,

Sebastian, you laughed the other night. I know for I saw you."

Seb took her arm to walk back to the kitchen wing. They were eating together, the four of them, and Meg insisted that under the circumstances it was easier for her to serve the meal in her own domain.

"May I bring Pete along when I come over for the hurricane? *If* the hurricane comes?" Ariana asked plaintively.

Meg was ladling onion soup. "You bring him," she assured Ariana, "for he'll need fresh water if the storm lasts a while, you know."

"Companionship, too," Seb said with a perfectly straight face. Ariana glanced at him and saw amusement in the blue eyes.

Luke said something to her just then, and she turned her head back hastily, and everyone was looking at her, waiting for her response. "I'm sorry," she stammered. "I was watching Seb and—"

Seb looked amused at that, and Luke asked again, "Will you be going to work tomorrow, honey? This storm is advancing with a vengeance."

Ariana looked out the window. "You think we'll get it, don't you, Luke?"

"Too soon to tell. I'm betting we'll be on the edge, that it'll come in somewhere just north of Miami. They're still saying Friday noon's the earliest for landfall in Florida, but the way Christine's picking up forward speed, we may soon hear some changes in that advisory, too."

They had reached the dessert stage, and Ariana got up to help Meg clear the table. "I'll be going to work, at least for the early morning, maybe longer, but isn't there something I should be doing for La Casita?"

Seb had turned on a transistor radio to pick up the 9 P.M. advisory. "We'll take care of your cottage, Ariana. Just see that you get yourself home in plenty of time. Phone me as soon as you get in, and I'll come down and help you with Pete."

Meg reminded her, "Bring along a change of clothes and something to read, too, to occupy the time."

Ariana felt Seb's eyes on her and flushed. "How many coffees?" she asked quickly, and poured out for four, taking the cups to the table as Meg served generous slices of freshly-baked mango pie.

Luke refused the beverage. "Never drink coffee this late," he apologized. "I'd not sleep at all."

Ariana regarded him with surprise. "Oh, sorry, I thought you said yes when I asked."

Meg gave her a sideways glance and assured her that it didn't matter. "I'll drink it. I like two cups of coffee with my pie." She patted Ariana's hand. "You put me in mind of dear Margaret so often. She was a little deaf, too."

"Aunt Margaret was deaf?" Astonishment showed in Ariana's lovely face. "I don't remember that."

"Not all deaf, never that," Meg said hastily.

Seb was looking quizzically at the puzzled girl. "You missed the operative word, Ariana. Meg said that Margaret was deaf *too.*"

"Oh, but I—" *Deaf?* She felt shattered. She put her pie fork carefully down on the plate. "Is this true?" she asked Seb, looking straight into his eyes.

"Darling," he said urgently, reaching for her, gathering her protectively into his arms. Somehow Meg and Luke melted away then, and they were alone in the kitchen. Seb's mouth came down, closing over hers—possessively, passionately—in kisses that left her breathless.

"My God, I've been waiting for that for hours," he said somewhat later, framing her face with strong hands. "I love you, woman." He buried his face in the soft bareness of her throat. "You always smell so delicious."

"Seb," she protested, fighting free of his embrace, "you said deaf *too.* You meant me, you know you did."

"Oh, that," he said in a dismissive sort of way and reached for her again.

"Yes, that!"

He poured fresh coffee for them, made her sit down, and then told her: "From what I've observed," he said, "I'd wager you have some conductive hearing loss, probably a genetic trait, a family weakness, for Margaret had it, too." Leaning over, he kissed the top of her nose. "What's a faulty ear or two? Some fourteen million Americans have a hearing problem of one kind or another." Curious, he asked her, "No one out in Colorado ever suggested that you were having difficulty hearing them? That Denver man never asked?"

She shook her head, her brown eyes bleak. "I thought only old people got deaf, Seb."

"Sometimes it comes on at a fairly early age, sometimes in the fifties. It all depends on the kind of problem causing the hearing loss. Sometimes the hearing loss is so sudden that the person seeks immediate help, and then occasionally it occurs so gradually, as yours probably did, maybe over a couple of months, perhaps over a couple of years, that the individual seldom tumbles to what's wrong. Usually someone else has to notice the problem.

"If it's in one ear only, unbalanced hearing results. I'm no ear specialist, Ariana, but I'd say that might be your problem. You weren't having a breakdown in Colorado, sweetheart, you were simply fighting to hear, misunderstanding some things and missing one hell of a lot of others."

She sat there, shocked. "Are you saying, Seb, that when I goofed so badly at Montval—?"

"Listen to these words, darling. Fifteen—fifty . . . September—December . . . nine—five. Hear how alike they sound? With a hearing loss, those sounds, and a thousand others, would be difficult to differentiate. When you told me about it, the night of the turtle hatching, you mentioned those specific words and I started to wonder. It explained a lot of things, like the times you were startled when you didn't hear me walk up close to you, questions you sometimes ignored, and times you asked for a repeat of what had just been said."

She sat thinking, her hands held tightly in his firm ones. "That's perhaps why I didn't hear the taxi coming, I suppose, isn't it, Seb? But I can *hear,* that's what's so hard to understand about this."

"Of course you can hear. But you're not picking up all the sounds within a normal frequency range. And that can be dangerous, as you just mentioned when you and the taxi collided. And it can make a demanding job with a lot of people-contact extremely difficult to do."

She looked so forlorn. Seb groaned and scooped her up in his arms again. "Darling, it's not the end of the world. I know an otologist, a splendid ear man in Coral Gables. He'll know what to do. It can be treated surgically, you know. Quite successfully, too."

She leaned against him, her cheek close against his shoulder. "I love you, Seb. What is it called?"

"Otosclerosis. It can be present at any age. That coffee's stone cold, darling. Here, let me take it. A bit of brandy, I think—settle you down and help you sleep." His blue eyes were tender. "Ready to go and say goodnight to Meg and Luke?"

She had herself under control now. "Yes, please. I don't want Meg feeling bad about this, Seb. It's better that I know, isn't it?"

He looked down at her as she stood close at his side. "Yes, although I didn't plan it quite that way, my darling. I thought you had enough adjustment to handle for a while. But don't worry about Meg—I saw her expression when I took you in my arms, and there was pure jubilation there!"

Her face was all rosy confusion at that. Seb's lips twitched. He said huskily, "My dearest dear," and he bent to kiss her.

She would remember this moment all her life—the tenderness of his gentle kisses, the quickening winds, and the feeling of being at home in Seb's arms.

*

Far to the south, Hurricane Christine picked up new speed, pounding on course through the Great Bahama Bank with savage, churning winds and frenzied seas.

CHAPTER 11

The insistent ring of the alarm clock penetrated Ariana's dreams. It had taken a long time to get to sleep last night, and now she reached out a shapely arm and groped drowsily for the clock's silencer. "Darn that—"

"Darn that old alarm clock!"

The voice, still fuzzy with sleep, was her own but it came from Pete's cage in the living room.

A startled smile curved her lips. "Hello, Pete! So that's what I sound like first thing in the morning?"

"Hello, Radnor! Have a cuppa tea."

She told him, "You're an old fraud, do you know that, Pete? You converse better than a heap of people I know." The parrot was singing softly as she started for the bathroom.

Seb telephoned while she was making coffee. The early advisories had him alarmed. Christine was boiling over open water again, with Bimini dead ahead. Landfall on the Florida coast was bound to be earlier than predicted yesterday, Seb said. "We'll get your shutters up first thing this morning. Promise me you'll come home before noon."

"Any other news?" she asked hesitantly.

"I love you," he told her. "Remember that. And for God's sake, drive carefully. The roads will be a madhouse."

They were, too—with people driving to work and from work and over to lumberyards for boarding-up plywood and in to the gas stations and grocery stores and then home again. "I got the very last loaf of bread at the Quik-Stoppe," Elena told her. "They are all out of candles."

Elena was friendlier to her these days. The Cuban girl was feeling more sure of Carlos, and it had made a difference in her attitude toward Ariana. There were only two customers browsing around the gift shop this morning, and few more expected. "Go and visit with Mr. Ferguson," Elena suggested. "I can handle things here."

Ariana ran over to the lounge, splashing through rain puddles, feeling the soaked earth squelch beneath her feet. Lately, she thought, she seemed always to be rushing, unable to settle, tense over Seb's precarious situation.

Florence had sandwiches and a pot of coffee going all the time now, for Paradise was working with a reduced crew doing the last of the boarding-up, and the men, weary and wet, came in as they could. Carlos was there, barefoot and in soaked trousers. He looked as tired as Ariana had ever seen him, going over the check-off lists with the men, dismissing them to go home when he was satisfied that all that was humanly possible to do in each area had been done.

"We're nearly all set here," he said wearily. "Why don't you get on home, Ariana."

Mr. Ferguson was concerned about her, too. "Will it be safe so close to the ocean? Why not stay here with us?"

She would be with friends, she assured him, people who had been through hurricanes before, and they'd leave for higher ground if the warnings came. "Maybe you know them," she said, staring straight at Carlos. "Sebastian Farleigh over at St. James Court?"

Just then Florence came out with fresh coffee. She took one look at Ariana. "How'd you get so wet? Catch your death of cold, you will, running around like that." There had been a phone call for Ariana a half hour ago, she added, wrapping a towel turban-fashion around the honey-blonde head.

"Who was it?" Ariana asked, tucking loose strands of damp hair under the towel.

"Someone in Colorado. Seemed to think we were all going to take wing and vanish out to sea with the storm winds." Florence sniffed. "Said her name was Lucy, and I was to tell you she's getting married next week."

"Wonderful! That's Lucy Welles. She's from Nassau, too, Florence."

"Is that a fact." Florence was unimpressed.

"She's marrying an Air Force captain, Stuart Rolle, an instructor in the U.S. Air Force Academy out in Colorado. He's from Nassau, too."

"Well!" Florence poured coffee for newly arrived Freddy and Armando. "Wish I'd known. Kinfolk, all of us Porters and Rolles. I knew Stu when he was breeches-high to a sand crab. Your hair's dry, Ariana. Finish up your coffee and get on home."

Mr. Ferguson nodded. "They'll soon be raising the highway bridges to let the boats come up to safe harbor. Car traffic backs up solid then. Go now while you can."

Ariana put down her cup, and the morning newspaper was right there on the table, and the lines leaped out at her: "Freighter and crew of eleven seized in marijuana raid. New DEA strike force intensifies search of small-harbor inlets along South Florida coastline . . ." She gave a little cry and looked up to see Freddy observing her.

"Christine's clobbered Bimini," Freddy said to all of them. "Now she's veering slightly east." Ariana drew in her breath, sharply. The parrot trainer touched her lightly on the arm. "What's the matter?" he asked quietly, turning a little so they stood apart from the others.

"That couple yesterday—did you find out what they were doing here at Paradise?"

Freddie shrugged. "I never did get the chance to check around, Radnor."

She looked at him, puzzled. "But you talked to them. I saw you—"

His face sobered. "When?"

"Right after the morning parrot show. I came back in because it was raining so hard and I saw them at the show, and they stopped on their way out and—"

"You still here?" Carlos interrupted. "Ariana, this is an order. Get going!"

She waved and gave them all a wide grin. "See you after the storm. Take care."

Freddy caught up with her before she reached her car. "Got a minute? We could use an extra pair of hands with the birds, if you can spare the time. Won't take more than another quarter hour, and it would help us stay on schedule."

She was glad to help, sitting with a towel covering her lap to swathe and hold the African Grey parrot whose claws Ken wanted to clip. Ken used a special nail clipper, working carefully while Ariana gripped the bird.

This parrot, Freddy's assistant explained, had been purchased recently as a mate for Pete. "It's a mature female," Ken said. "At least we think she's a female. Mr. Ferguson's named her Amy."

"Surname Lowell," Ariana laughed. She shifted the towel carefully, isolating the bird's other foot for Ken to work on, and wondered where Freddy had gone.

Ken told her that it was thought by some authorities that King Solomon, of Biblical times, kept tamed African Greys. "England's Henry the Eighth, too," he said. "Between wives, no doubt. But it is a known fact that King Henry had an African Grey as a pet."

Ariana stole a glance at her watch. Eleven-thirty. Seb would be livid. "As soon as you're done with Amy's nails I've got to go."

Ken walked her back to the yellow VW. "Is it always this dark before a hurricane?" she fretted.

Ken didn't know. He was from South Dakota, and this was his first tropical storm. "Most of the grounds crew were predicting Christine would hit before tomorrow morning, though," he ventured, looking up at the darkening sky and the low cloud masses scudding toward the north. "Keep your transistor radio tuned in to the latest advisories, Ariana. The weather warning system's mighty good, they tell me."

Hers was one of the last cars to cross over the inlet bridge before the gates came down, temporarily closing the highway, and the bridge span was elevated. A flotilla of boats of all sizes streamed through on their way to inland harborage—white yachts, tall masted sailboats, shrimpers, day cruisers. All sought safety from the high seas and the devastating winds.

Ariana stopped in Hibiscus to pick up her mail. She bought the last flashlight batteries the general store still had, and drove on with rain pounding down on her little car.

The winds were very brisk now, whipping the tortured palms, bending the oaks and pines. Fallen leaves and bits of paper and street debris blew against her windshield. Although the hurricane itself was still hours off, it was time to take cover.

She reached home, grateful to have arrived safely and terribly uneasy about the strangely darkened day. Sheets of rain engulfed her as she stepped gingerly from the VW, avoiding the puddles.

She never heard a sound as the two men closed in, but her eye caught a shadowed movement and she swung around to face the rat-faced man. She gave a sobbing, smothered cry. Behind her, someone seized her arms, and a familiar voice said, "You little snoop! You just had to meddle, didn't you?"

The vicious blow struck the back of her head. The breath went out of her in a small sigh. She crumpled forward to the wet ground, fading rapidly into unconsciousness, hearing disjointed fragments— ". . . the cocaine . . . just another hurricane death . . ."

She lay still, alone, no longer aware of the turbulent

winds nor feeling the deepening pool of rain water that engulfed her chin and spread slowly, fatally, toward her nostrils—

*

By twelve Seb had made his second fruitless trip to La Casita, pounding on the dutch door while his raincoat billowed out from his body. Rain stung his tense face as he fought his way back against the wind.

"She's still not home?" Meg asked, tight-lipped with concern as she met him at the door.

He shook his head and shrugged out of the yellow stormcoat. "I'll try calling Paradise again. Perhaps they've heard something by now. Meg, maybe the men are ready for lunch."

The two men waiting in the living room politely refused Meg's offer of food. The short, dark-haired one rose heavily from his armchair and stood listening at Seb's side as he dialed the gardens. Seb spoke with both James Ferguson and Carlos. There was no news at Paradise, they assured him. They had sent Ariana on her way considerably before twelve o'clock, and she should have reached home almost an hour ago.

"Wait a minute," Carlos said. "Someone's just come in— hey, Ken, have you seen anything of Ariana?"

Seb clutched the receiver with white-knuckled fingers, waiting. "Sorry," Carlos came back on to say. "No one here knows anything more, Dr. Farleigh. Ken wondered if she got across before the bridge went up that first time. You'll keep in touch with us, please?"

Seb went back to pacing the floor.

The tall black man in the well-tailored Palm Beach suit stirred uneasily in his chair. "You're absolutely certain she's not in the cottage, Seb? Luke and I could take off one of the aluminum shutters and climb in, check the place over."

"There's no one there but that damn parrot," Seb muttered, flicking on the switch that controlled the listening device concealed near the fireplace in La Casita. "Listen to him—he's been enough to drive us out of our minds!"

Pete's voice came through, loud and clear. "Hello, Freddy! Hello, Freddy! Call the cops. Call the cops."

Seb winced. "See what I mean?"

The short man grimaced. "Relax, friend, you're wearing out the carpet, and that kind does not grow on palm trees." Again he heaved himself out of the deep lounge chair. "Cut the bird off. I can't stand him either. Wesley, any ideas?"

The black man nodded. "Time to search. Something's gone wrong. The telephones are still working; she'd have phoned in by now if it were car trouble."

"Call the cops!" Pete shouted. "Hello, Freddy!"

Seb's hand was reaching for the switch when he suddenly froze. His blue eyes narrowed. "My God!" he cried, pushing past Luke, flinging open the door and shouldering his way into the storm.

Wes Sutherland caught up with him at the terrace edge, and the two men pounded on down the drive. Far behind puffed the short, dark-haired man and Luke. Through wildly waving shrubbery, Seb caught a glimpse of yellow that could only be Ariana's car and vaulted a fence to reach the spot more quickly.

They saw her then, a fragile fallen figure, her head in the shallow pool of water and her long bright hair dark now with blood and rain—lying so still, so quiet, so icy-cold.

*

Somewhere far away a voice was calling, echoing in the chambers of her brain and begging her to breathe. Oh God, the pain of it—the agony of her head, the swordlike pain in her lungs . . .

Someone said, "She's breathing on her own, Seb. Give over, man."

A woman's tearful voice speaking of blankets and a bed, and then she was coughing, gasping, and her lungs were fire, but she was breathing. Breathing again—fighting for life—breathing—

"Oh my God, darling"—and that strangely reverent voice was Seb's, and he was holding her close, but carefully—so carefully—and her head was a mass of pain and bandages.

"Seb?"

"Yes, darling. You're all right, Ariana. You're safe, my darling."

She opened puzzled brown eyes. Her own living room . . . her own sofa . . . A little ghost of a smile touched her pallid face, and she fought free of the blankets. "Please, I want to—to sit up."

Seb cradled her in his arms, elevating her just a little. The sound of wind drifted in to the shuttered room. She saw the two men watching her, and one was the swarthy stranger she had seen once before in the living room at the Court. Everything came flooding back—every memory.

She took a painful breath, eyes frightened, the smile stiffening on her lips. And she knew she could not be a part of it any longer. Not even if she died for it.

Her voice was hoarse, weary, and she pressed herself wretchedly back against the brocade cushions. "Seb, I love you. I'll love you forever. But I can't keep quiet any longer about the drugs, Seb."

The short, dark man came out of his chair in a kind of lunging motion, and Ariana's eyes closed in panic. She said, unsteadily, "Your friends may as well kill me now, Seb, for I'm going to get up off this sofa and telephone the police."

"We're already here, Miss Radnor," the swarthy man said quietly.

Color rushed to her pale cheeks. "You—"

He bowed slightly. "Sal Buntemundo, Bunte to my

friends, of the federal Drug Enforcement Administration." He indicated the black man, who smiled warmly at her. "Wesley Sutherland of U.S. Customs. And I believe you are already well acquainted with the gentleman who holds you in his arms, our friend 'Tian, on temporary assignment to the DEA's special task force."

From Pete's covered cage came a muffled protest. Take one thing at a time, Ariana told herself. One thing at a time. "Please—Seb, is this true?"

He said huskily, holding her, "It's true, and you're going to marry me, aren't you?"

She nodded, winced, and drew a shaky breath. "So your friend Bunte, the—ah—pilot with the lousy night schedule who almost slept in my bedroom, is really a DEA agent? Then who hit me on the head? It was Carlos, wasn't it? I thought I recognized his voice. Carlos and that rat-faced man—they were talking about cocaine when they struck me." She wailed, "And I liked Carlos."

Seb looked astounded. "Carlos? Never Carlos, darling. You'd be surprised to know how Carlos has been helping us. It was Freddy Messina, the parrot trainer. They thought you'd overheard them, you see, yesterday at the trained bird show. And the rat-faced man, as you call him, gave Freddy orders to eliminate you." He kissed her forehead. "They came up to the cottage after they had slugged you, and old Pete there tipped me off as they unlocked the door with your key. When we finally tumbled to what was happening, it was action *fast*. They heard us coming and tried to get away." He said wonderingly, "Nobody is faster with a gun than Wes."

Wes Sutherland inserted, "Messina is the 'E.M.' we've been looking for, Miss Radnor. Recently we got a lead—no matter how we got it—and found out only the initials of a name, but weren't aware until he ambushed you that the man we were after was this same Freddy."

She said emphatically, "E.M.? But then it can't be

Freddy, can it?" Curious, she asked, "What was I supposed to have overheard, for heaven's sake?"

Bunte told her. "Freddy is Elfredo Messina. *E.M.* He's a small but important part of a well-organized dope-smuggling ring, and it turns out that for the better part of the last six months he's been using the poker game with—er—a bird named Keats to signal dates to persons in the audience. Dates concerning various major shipments of drugs from what is called a 'mother ship.'"

"Oh." It was almost too much to fathom, and her head hurt, too. "I always thought he was Freddy for Frederico. I never heard a word they said to each other, you know that, Seb. And I just thought that Freddy had gotten Keats's cards mixed up, worrying about the hurricane."

Behind her she could hear Luke talking to Meg, and there was the pleasant rattle of dishes on a wheeled trolley. "Ah, yes," said Seb, "the hurricane. Christine's kicked up her heels again and turned strongly northeast."

Bunte muttered. "Hurricanes are unpredictable. So now she's off to Bermuda."

"We're getting no hurricane? No storm at all? After all that wind and rain?" She could hardly believe it.

Luke came over to the sofa with a cup of hot tea for her. "We have high winds and storm damage. We've gotten the edge of the blow, honey, but no hurricane. Not this one. Not unless she turns again."

They had brought lunch down from the Court, once they knew Ariana was going to be all right. And Bunte had called Paradise with the news. Meg looked over at her now. What was everyone thinking of, letting the girl lie there in her damp pant-suit? "She needs dry clothes, Sebastian," Meg snapped.

But there was still so much to be explained. "I'll wrap up in the blankets again," she compromised with them. "Just for a few minutes more. Then I'll change, Meg. I promise."

She was aching all over now, and her head throbbed, so

she asked quickly, "They knocked me unconscious and left me lying in a puddle of water, knowing I'd drown there as the water deepened, didn't they? I heard them say something about cocaine, and that I'd be found dead. 'She'll be just another hurricane death,' one of them said." She shuddered. "If you know it was Freddy, that means you caught them, doesn't it? Both of them?"

"Three of them," Wes Sutherland said confidently. "There was a woman waiting for them in a car beyond your main gate."

Bunte eyed the trays of chicken sandwiches, fruit salad, and Meg's chocolate cake with enthusiasm. "Two of the so-called 'cocaine cowboys' nabbed. Not a bad day's work, but it seems a shame to malign our Western folk heroes by calling these punks 'cowboys,' doesn't it? No self-respecting cowboy would ride herd with the likes of those men.

"Well, at any rate, thanks to Seb and a few others, we've caught two—maybe three. No kingpin yet, but just wait. The net draws a little tighter every day." He said with satisfaction, selecting a triple-decker chicken sandwich, "This time we've caught ourselves a squealer. Yes, sir, that Freddy's going to talk more than old Pete here. Right, 'Tian?"

Seb's handsome face grew still. "It appears so." He was thinking that it would be a long time before he would forget the terror in his heart when he saw the honey-blonde hair, darkened with blood and rain, floating so lifelessly in the pool of water.

He scooped Ariana up in his arms and strode off to the bedroom, calling for Meg to come and help. "You've had a whale of a blow on your head," he admonished her, "and we must keep close watch on something like that. Maybe x-rays will be needed, too. Right now I want you to let Meg help you take a warm bath and then get you to bed for a while. The men have to get back to make their reports, and I need to talk privately with them first. Will you rest now while I get our friends on their way?"

She clung to him. "It's over, though, isn't it? Your part in all this? You'll not go away, will you, Seb?"

Her lovely head was drooping with fatigue. He caught her face between the cool palms of his hands and kissed her gently. "I'll not leave you, and that's a promise, small one. Rest now. We'll talk again."

He looked at her and his deep blue eyes were deadly serious. "And I'll tell you one thing. You're having that ear surgery just as soon as I can arrange it. I won't have my wife getting conked on the head on the average of once a month!"

*

By sunset the rains ceased and the winds diminished. Seb took Ariana, in silk nightgown and warm robe, out to the cypress deck to watch the sky change from stormy gray to the orange- and rose-streaked banners of tropical sundown.

"Incredible, isn't it?" She turned to look at him, moving stiffly and very aware of the bandage covering part of her head. "So stormy this morning and now so beautiful a sunset."

"Beautiful," he echoed, but his eyes were on the girl at his side, seeing the color flood her pretty face at his words.

With a wry smile she touched the bandage. "Not like this."

He looked down at her, a promise of love in his eyes. "Any time, any way." It was a covenant beyond the hours of this confusing day.

They turned back toward the living room, and she asked, "Do you suppose Meg remembered to feed Pete? Poor Pete, you've left his cage covered for hours."

"I fed him," Seb said in a rather strange voice. "I can't stand the creature, but I'll be grateful to him every day of my life."

She remembered now what he had said before, and as he sank down in a deep armchair with her close in his arms, she asked: "You said earlier that Pete tipped you off. How on earth did that happen?"

His hands lingered on her sloping shoulders. Quietly he explained the listening device that Bunte had installed in La Casita while she had been having dinner at the Court.

"The night of the turtle hatching. I *knew* someone had been in here. But why, Seb? Surely you knew I had nothing to do with drugs."

His arm tightened about her as he explained how the remote cottage was originally part of the overall scheme to pinpoint the drug smugglers. "You really threw a spanner in the works, arriving when you did and then *staying on*. My God," Seb said, holding her close against his broad chest, "not only did you stay, you also found a job at Paradise. And by then we'd narrowed our search for the contact man with the drug ring down to four places—and Paradise was one of the four."

She saw the haggard look cross his face. "I was crazy with worry when you took that job at Paradise, my darling. I tried every way I could think of—"

She reached up and touched his lips. "I know. All those Miami job offers. The Coral Gables one, too. Were Tony and Drake helping Bunte, too?"

He drew a deep breath. "For such a little person, you certainly make waves, don't you? I told you what the bubba system was, Ariana. Suffice it to say there are also many intelligent, well-placed individuals, like Drake and Tony, who fight evil with every chance they get, working with DEA agents even to the point of endangering their own lives."

She leaned closer to the strength of him. "I think I understand, Seb. I'll forget I saw them with Bunte at the Court. That's what you mean, isn't it?"

"Yes, darling, that's what I mean." His eyes slid over her. "Fetching outfit," he said quietly, changing the subject. His mouth came down to hers, touching her lips in a tender caress.

"Seb," she protested, "you said you'd answer all my questions."

He lifted his dark head. "Still more questions?" he muttered grimly. "I want to make love to you, darling."

Everywhere he touched her a little fire started in her body. "Please," she begged. "I'm just beginning to see what this is all about. I understand now how you happened to arrive so cavalierly when I had Freddy over for supper. You were listening in, weren't you? And you heard Freddy—" She broke off, crimson with embarrassment.

Seb roared. "Yes, I did. I heard Freddy trying to make time with what I considered to be *my* lady." He sobered. "Mostly we just heard Pete. *Ad infinitum.* Luke and I, monitoring."

She gave him an oblique look. "Eavesdropping!"

"To protect you," he said quietly. "When all is said and done, I shouldn't be surprised if Freddy is found to have the blue macaws. Carlos thinks so, too. Carlos is buying into Paradise, you know—little by little, and with Ferguson's blessing." His hand stroked her cheek, slid to her throat, and she could feel the quiver through his body.

He said, "When I think of what Freddy did to you—"

"But I'm all right, darling." She turned so that she could see his eyes when she told him. "I know about the malpractice suit, Seb." She saw the handsome jaw go rigid, and explained hastily: "Meg thought I ought to know, and I'm glad she told me. But knowing about it somehow made me more unsure of you—of how you'd feel after something like that—and it seemed, somehow, so possible that you might have gotten into drugs. You had that expensive Lancia and—and other things."

Her voice faltered. "That wasn't easy to say, but I had to tell you. Forgive me for not trusting you, Seb."

She felt his lips on her eyelids, on the corners of her mouth. Protectively, his arms clasped her to him. "That's what you were supposed to think. You and everyone else. Part of the overall plan, darling."

"Why you?"

"Point one: I had a private inlet with rapid access to the sea, and a boat to match. Point two: the malpractice suit was common knowledge, and the DEA could capitalize on it, playing me up as a disgruntled physician in need of large sums of cash. A perfect setup."

She moved restlessly in his arms. "I heard the Seacraft go out so many times, always late at night. And you let me think you were in on the drug smuggling, you know you did. Even that night when I confronted you with what I knew—well, with what I *thought* I knew—even then you let me go on assuming that you were one of them."

"But I never actually lied to you, darling. Think back. I had to let you continue believing what you did, for your own safety and for the success of the undercover operation I've been part of.

"Drug smuggling is a sophisticated business these days, what with the inertial navigation systems available. Equipped with INS and having a computer and other electronic equipment, a drug-laden 'mother ship' can establish a fail-proof rendezvous at sea with one or more smaller delivery vessels—freighters, runabouts, yachts, what have you—a rendezvous anywhere and in any kind of weather. Unfortunately, it is also a wretched, illegal business that burns out human life.

"I only wish," Seb said earnestly, "that the teenager who considers marijuana harmless would read the scientific studies showing marijuana to be oil-soluble. And that means it is liable to remain within the human body for who knows how long, doing who knows how much future damage."

He shook his head, continuing, "And I most sincerely wish that every law-abiding college graduate who thinks cocaine is a sophisticated party treat could look over my shoulder at a newborn baby that cannot breathe properly because of its mother's drug addiction."

Ariana made a sad little sound, and Seb leaned down and kissed the tip of her nose. "And now I'm going to get some supper ready for us," he said. "Meg's left soup, avocado mousse, and lobster salad. Sound good?"

It sounded delicious. From the sofa she watched him set the cherry-wood table and warm the soup. Pete called out when he heard her voice, and Seb sighed and removed the cover from the bird's cage.

When they had eaten, he helped Ariana prepare for the night. Then he carried her through to her room and placed her gently down on the bed. Dusk had fallen. Through the open shutters came the night scent of tropical jasmine.

"It's nearly ten," Seb said quietly. He checked her pulse and the pupils of her eyes, and pulled the cool sheet up over the yellow silk of her gown. His lips sought hers in a tender kiss. "Mmm, you always smell delicious. Think you can get to sleep all right now?"

She whispered shakily, "Seb, must you go?" To waken in the night . . . to dream—Tears misted on her lashes.

He knelt beside her, burying his face in the fragrant curve of her throat. "Dear heart, I'm not leaving you. I promised, remember? You'll not be alone, small one. I'm going to be checking how you are about every ninety minutes right through the night. That blow on the head— we're taking no chances."

There was a mischievous twinkle in her eyes. "All night? What will Meg and Luke think about that?"

He bent over her, and she felt his mouth touch hers, and the kiss was fire and longing, goodness and grace. When he released her, he murmured huskily, "They will think that I trust no one but myself to safeguard my future wife, dear love."

She said shakily, "That sounds wonderful. When, Seb?"

"We'll get the license tomorrow." He watched the

lashes flicker down against her cheeks. "I'm not waiting an hour beyond the legal time limit for you. Sunday night you'll sleep in my arms."

"And tonight?" she asked worriedly. "Seb, you've had a wretched day, too. You can't sit up all night because of me."

"Luke's brought down my robe. I'll have a shower and settle down on the sofa. Don't fret, I'll be fine."

She clung to him, wanting his kisses, and his mouth moved over her face, caressing her eyes and her chin and the little hollows in her cheeks. "Love. Dear love," he murmured. "I'll come back in to kiss you goodnight."

A moment later she heard the sound of the shower, and then the growling noise that Pete made when he was restless or lonely.

"Pete," she called out to him, "go to sleep. I'll see you in the morning."

The parrot was singing to her. Ariana raised her head. She held her breath, listening to the words. Perfectly in tune came the sound of the song:

> Moon over Miami,
> Shine on my love and me—

She cried out, "Seb! Did you hear that? He's singing his theme song. Oh, Pete, you old darling, you did it! You really did it!"

"Honey," Seb said, and his voice held suppressed laughter, "this you'll have to see to believe." He came into the bedroom, tying the belt of his short terry robe, moisture from the shower still on his dark hair. He lifted her up in his arms and walked back to the parrot's cage.

"Congratulations are in order," Seb said.

"He deserves it," she agreed. "Two whole lines—wasn't he splendid?"

"Look a little closer," Seb suggested, and then, of course, she saw what Seb meant. On the floor of Pete's cage lay a single white egg about one and one-half inches long.

"Oh . . . Pete."

Seb covered the cage. "Goodnight, Petra," he said firmly, and carried Ariana back to bed.

She was weak with laughter. "Don't go," she begged him. "Please don't go." She stroked his hair and touched his face. Tears slid down her cheeks.

Seb switched off the bedside light. With a hoarse sound deep in his throat, he lay down beside her and took her in his arms, gentling her, comforting her. "This has been one hell of a day. You're all unstrung. Stop weeping now or I shall have to give you something to quiet you, darling."

She swallowed a sob. "How strange—part laughter, part tears." She moved closer, her head nestling into the curve of his broad shoulder. "Seb?"

"Hmm?"

She wished she could see his face. "Will you be going back into medicine now?"

His arm tightened about her. "I've never really left it. Yes, I plan to go into practice again—right here, as a matter of fact. Would you like that?"

Happiness flooded through her. "Yes, I would. We'd live in the Court, wouldn't we? You and I and Meg and Luke—"

"And the children when we have them, about three, wouldn't you say? But not Petra."

He was laughing at her, and she didn't mind. She wiggled her toes, thinking. "Seb, what about La Casita?"

"Always your bolthole," he said drowsily. "Margaret knew what she was doing."

She let out her breath in a tiny sigh of satisfaction. "Yes, she did, didn't she? Seb, why don't we invite Lucy and Stu to use it for their honeymoon?"

"Good idea. Call her tomorrow and suggest it. Go to sleep now." His voice was soothing, and his lips lightly brushed her forehead.

Ariana lifted her arms and nibbled Seb's ear. "Oh, I love you so much."

She was quite unprepared for what happened next. Seb groaned and his mouth came down upon hers, drifting from her lips to her chin, down her slender throat and back to her mouth in deeply possessive kisses, urgent in his need of her.

"Darling, my darling," he muttered, his hands gentle on her breasts, touching them, kissing them, while a tremor shuddered through her. She clung to him, her hands warm on his cool body.

"You're beautiful—so beautiful." His voice held a husky sound. "Darling, I want you—I love you—"

Abruptly, he released her, left the bed, and turned on the dresser lamp. Bewildered, she cried out to him, "Seb?"

He reached down and pulled up the sheet to cover the softly rounded young body. "No," he said firmly. "Not tonight, my little witch. I love you, Ariana. I love your wanting me, I love the feel of your hands on my skin. I love to kiss you, to touch you—my God, darling, it's hard to wait for you. But—"

He sat down on the edge of the bed and tilted up her chin with one lean, firm hand. Their eyes met, hers uncertain, his deep, loving blue.

He asked, "Do you remember the other night we were together, here on this bed? The night you told me I would be the first? I said then that that night was for promises, my darling girl." His lips came to hers in a gentle kiss. "We'll soon be lovers, together in every sense of the word. And when I make you mine, dear heart, it is going to be a wondrous union, unhampered by head bandages and ninety-minute pupil checks."

He looked down at her, his eyes dark with love. "Understand, darling?"

She put out a hand to touch his dear face. "Oh, yes.

Tonight—"

He caught her fingers and pressed them to his lips. "Tonight, beloved, is for cherishing."

Outside, a crescent of new moon appeared in the sky from behind a bank of clouds. The scent of frangipani and star jasmine drifted across the gardens of the Court, and the ocean returned once more to a gently creaming surf.